"The feelings arousec
widely as the settings
Africa and China . .
penned anything so s
"The Luncheon" . . . Amazingly different is "The First Miracle" . . . 11 RIVETING TALES THAT COULD HAVE BEEN INVENTED ONLY BY THE AUTHOR OF *KANE & ABEL* AND *THE PRODIGAL DAUGHTER* . . ."

—Publishers Weekly

"Ironic twists and carefully constructed surprises . . . IN THE STANDOUT "OLD LOVE" . . . ARCHER'S STYLE IS DISPLAYED TO GREATEST ADVANTAGE, BRILLIANTLY UNDERSTANDING THE STRENGTH OF THE BONDS OF LOVE."

—Library Journal

"Engaging . . . genuine surprises . . . ARCHER DELIVERS . . . WITH GLOSSY PROFESSIONALISM"

—Kirkus Reviews

"The tales are studded with exotic information . . . Each story ends with a twist ranging from the wry to the sardonic."

—Boston Sunday Globe

"A FORMIDABLE TALENT . . . IN THIS SHORT STORY COLLECTION, THE AUTHOR OF *KANE & ABEL* AND *THE PRODIGAL DAUGHTER* PROVES HIS MASTERY OF THE SHORT STORY FORM."

—Sacramento Union

Books by Jeffrey Archer

The Prodigal Daughter
A Quiver Full of Arrows

Published by POCKET BOOKS NEW YORK

PUBLISHED BY POCKET BOOKS NEW YORK

Originally published in Great Britain in 1980
by Hodder and Stoughton

POCKET BOOKS, a division of Simon & Schuster, Inc.
1230 Avenue of the Americas, New York, N.Y. 10020

Published by arrangement with Linden Press/Simon & Schuster
Library of Congress Catalog Card Number: 82-12707

ISBN: 0-671-45686-5

First Pocket Books printing July, 1983

10 9 8 7 6 5 4 3 2 1

Printed in the U.S.A.

To Victoria

AUTHOR'S NOTE

Of these eleven short stories, ten are based on known incidents (some embellished with considerable license). Only one is totally the result of my own imagination.

"The Luncheon" was inspired by W. Somerset Maugham.

J.A.

Contents

A
QUIVER
FULL OF
ARROWS

The Chinese Statue

THE LITTLE CHINESE STATUE was the next item to come under the auctioneer's hammer. Lot 103 caused those quiet murmurings that always precede the sale of a masterpiece. The auctioneer's assistant held up the delicate piece of ivory for the packed audience to admire while the auctioneer glanced around the room to be sure he knew where the serious bidders were seated. I studied my catalogue and read the detailed description of the piece, and what was known of its history.

The statue had been purchased in Ha Li Chuan in 1871 and was referred to as what Sotheby's quaintly described as "the property of a gentleman," usually meaning that some member of the aristocracy did not wish to admit that he was having to sell off one of the family heirlooms. I wondered if that was the case on this occasion and decided to do some research to discover what had caused the little Chinese statue to find its way into the auction rooms on that Thursday morning more than one hundred years later.

"Lot Number 103," declared the auctioneer. "What am I bid for this magnificent example of . . .?"

• • •

Sir Alexander Heathcote, as well as being a gentleman, was an exact man. He was exactly six feet three and a quarter inches tall, rose at seven o'clock every morning, joined his wife at breakfast to eat one boiled egg cooked for precisely four minutes and two pieces of toast with one spoonful of Cooper's marmalade and drink one cup of China tea. He would then take a hackney carriage from his flat in Cadogan Gardens at exactly eight-twenty and arrive at the Foreign Office at promptly eight fifty-nine, to return home again on the stroke of six o'clock.

Sir Alexander had been exact from an early age, as became the only son of a general. But unlike his father, he chose to serve his Queen in the diplomatic service, another exacting calling. He progressed from a shared desk at the Foreign Office in Whitehall to third secretary in Calcutta, to second secretary in Vienna, to first secretary in Rome, to Deputy Ambassador in Washington, and finally to minister in Peking. He was delighted when Mr. Gladstone invited him to represent the government in China, as he had for some considerable time taken more than an amateur interest in the art of the Ming dynasty. This crowning appointment in his distinguished career would afford him what until then he would have considered impossible—an opportunity to observe in their natural habitat some of the great statues, paintings and drawings that he had previously been able to admire only in books.

When Sir Alexander arrived in Peking, after a journey by sea and land that took his party nearly two months, he presented his seals patent to the Empress Tzu-Hsi and a personal letter for her private reading from Queen Victoria. The Empress, dressed from head to toe in white and gold, received her new Ambassador in the throne room of the Imperial Palace. She read the letter from the British monarch while Sir Alexander remained standing to attention. Her Imperial Highness revealed nothing of its contents to the new minister, only wishing him a successful term of office in his appointment. She then moved her lips slightly up at the corners, which Sir Alexander judged correctly to mean that the audience had come to an end. As he was conducted back through the great halls of the Imperial Palace by a mandarin in the long court dress of black and gold, Sir Alexander walked as slowly as possible, taking in the magnificent collection of ivory and jade statues scattered casually around the building much in the way Cellini and Michelangelo today lie stacked against each other in Florence.

As his ministerial appointment was for only three years, Sir Alexander took no leave, preferring to use his time to put the Embassy behind him and travel on horseback into the outlying districts to learn more about the country and its people. On these trips he was always accompanied by a mandarin from the palace staff who acted as interpreter and guide.

On one such journey, passing through the muddy streets of a small village with but a few houses called Ha Li Chuan, a distance of some fifty miles from Peking, Sir Alexander chanced upon an old craftsman's working place. Leaving his servants, the minister dismounted from his horse and entered the ramshackle wooden workshop to admire the delicate pieces of ivory and jade that crammed the shelves from floor to ceiling. Although modern, the pieces were superbly executed by an experienced craftsman and the minister entered the little hut with the thought of acquiring a small memento of his journey. Once in the shop he could hardly move in any direction for fear of knocking something over. The building had not been designed for a six-foot-three-and-a-quarter visitor. Sir Alexander stood still, quite enthralled, taking in the fine scented jasmine smell that hung in the air.

An old craftsman bustled forward in a long blue coolie robe and flat black hat to greet him; a jet-black plaited pigtail fell down his back. He bowed very low and then looked up at the giant from England. The minister returned the bow while the mandarin explained who Sir Alexander was and his desire to be allowed to look at the work of the craftsman. The old man was nodding his agreement even before the mandarin had come to the end of his request. For over an hour the minister sighed and chuckled as he studied many of the pieces with admiration and finally returned to the old man to praise his skill. The craftsman bowed once again and his shy smile revealed no teeth but only genuine pleasure at Sir Alexander's compliments. Pointing a finger to the back of the shop, he beckoned the two important visitors to follow him. They did so and entered a veritable Aladdin's cave, with row upon row of beautiful miniature emperors and classical figures. The minister could have happily settled down in the orgy of ivory for at least a week. Sir Alexander and the craftsman chatted away to each other through the interpreter, and the minister's love and knowledge of the Ming dynasty was soon revealed. The little craftsman's face lit up with this discovery and he turned to the mandarin and in a hushed voice made a request. The mandarin nodded his agreement and translated.

"I have, Your Excellency, a piece of Ming myself that you might care to see. A statue that has been in my family for over seven generations."

"I should be honored," said the minister.

"It is I who would be honored, Your Excellency," said the little man, who thereupon scampered out of the back door, nearly falling over a stray dog, and on to an old peasant house a few yards behind the workshop. The minister and the mandarin remained in the back room, for Sir Alexander knew that the old man would never have considered inviting an honored guest into his humble home until they had known each other for many years, and only then after he had been invited to Sir Alexander's home first. A few minutes passed before the little blue figure came trotting back, pigtail bouncing up and down on his shoulders. He was now clinging to something that, from the very way he held it close to his chest, had to be a treasure. The craftsman passed the piece over for the minister to study. Sir Alexander's mouth opened wide and he could not hide his excitement. The little statue, no more than six inches in height, was of the Emperor Kung and as fine an example of Ming as the minister had ever seen. Sir Alexander felt confident that the maker was the great Pen Q, who had been patronized by the Emperor, so that the date must have been around the turn of the fifteenth century. The statue's only blemish was that the ivory base on which such pieces usually rest was missing, and a small stick protruded from the bottom of the imperial robes; but in the eyes of Sir Alexander nothing could detract from its overall beauty. Although the craftsman's lips did not move, his eyes glowed with the pleasure his guest evinced as he studied the ivory Emperor.

"You think the statue is good?" asked the craftsman through the interpreter.

"It's magnificent," the minister replied. "Quite magnificent."

"My own work is not worthy to stand by its side," the craftsman added humbly.

"No, no," said the minister, though in truth the little craftsman knew that the great man was only being kind, for Sir Alexander was holding the ivory statue in a way that already showed the same love as the old man had for the piece.

The minister smiled down at the craftsman as he handed back the Emperor Kung and then he uttered perhaps the only undiplomatic words he had ever spoken in thirty-five years of serving his Queen and country.

"How I wish the piece was mine."

Sir Alexander regretted voicing his thoughts immediately he heard the mandarin translate them, because he knew only too well the old Chinese tradition that if an honored guest requests something, the giver will grow in the eyes of his fellow men by parting with it.

A sad look came over the face of the little old craftsman as he handed the figurine back to the minister.

"No, no. I was only joking," said Sir Alexander, quickly trying to return the piece to its owner.

"You would dishonor my humble home if you did not take the Emperor, Your Excellency," the old man said anxiously and the mandarin gravely nodded his agreement.

The minister remained silent for some time. "I have dishonored my own home, sir," he replied, and looked toward the mandarin, who remained inscrutable.

The little craftsman bowed. "I must fix a base on the statue," he said, "or you will not be able to put the piece on view."

He went to a corner of the room and opened a wooden packing chest that must have housed a hundred bases for his own statues. Rummaging around, he picked out a base decorated with small dark figures that the minister did not care for but that nevertheless made a perfect fit; the old man assured Sir Alexander that although he did not know the base's history, the piece bore the mark of a good craftsman.

The embarrassed minister took the gift and tried hopelessly to thank the little old man. The craftsman once again bowed low as Sir Alexander and the expressionless mandarin left the little workshop.

As the party traveled back to Peking, the mandarin observed the terrible state the minister was in, and uncharacteristically spoke first:

"Your Excellency is no doubt aware," he said, "of the old Chinese custom that when a stranger has been generous, you must return the kindness within the calendar year."

Sir Alexander smiled his thanks and thought carefully about the mandarin's words. Once back in his official residence, he went immediately to the Embassy's extensive library to see if he could discover a realistic value for the little masterpiece. After much diligent research, he came across a drawing of a Ming statue that was almost an exact copy of the one now in his possession and with the help of the mandarin he was able to assess its true worth, a figure that came to almost three years' emolument for a servant of the Crown. The minister discussed the problem with Lady Heathcote and she left her husband in no doubt as to the course of action he must take.

The following week the minister dispatched a letter by private messenger to his bankers, Coutts & Company, in the Strand, London, requesting that they send a large part of his savings to reach him in Peking as quickly as possible. When the funds arrived nine weeks later, the minister again approached the mandarin, who listened to his questions and, seven days later, gave him the details he had asked for.

The mandarin had discovered that the little craftsman, Yung Lee, came from the old and trusted family of Yung Shau, who had for some five hundred years been craftsmen. Sir Alexander also learned that many of Yung Lee's ancestors had examples of their work in the palaces of the Manchu princes. Yung Lee himself was growing old and wished to retire to the hills above the village, where his ancestors had always died. His son was ready to take over the workshop from him and continue the family tradition. The minister thanked the mandarin for his diligence and had only one more request of him. The mandarin listened sympathetically to the Ambassador from England and returned to the palace to seek advice.

A few days later the Empress granted Sir Alexander's request.

Almost a year to the day, the minister, accompanied by the mandarin, set out again from Peking for the village of Ha Li Chuan. When Sir Alexander arrived he immediately dismounted from his horse and entered the workshop that he remembered so well. The old man was seated at his bench, his flat hat slightly askew, a piece of uncarved ivory held lovingly between his fingers. He looked up from his work and shuffled toward the minister, not recognizing his guest until he could almost touch the foreign giant. Then he bowed low. The minister spoke through the mandarin:

"I have returned, sir, within the calendar year to repay my debt."

"There was no need, Your Excellency. My family is honored that the little statue lives in a great Embassy and may one day be admired by the people of your own land."

The minister could think of no words to form an adequate reply and simply requested that the old man should accompany him on a short journey.

The craftsman agreed without question and the three men set out on donkeys toward the north. They traveled for over two hours up a thin winding path into the hills behind the craftsman's workshop, and when they reached the village of Ma Tien they were met by another mandarin, who bowed low to the minister and requested that Sir Alexander and the craftsman continue their journey with him on foot. They walked in silence to the far side of the village and stopped only when they had reached a hollow in the hill from which there was a magnificent view of the valley all the way down to Ha Li Chuan. In the hollow stood a newly completed small white house of the most perfect proportions. Two stone lion-dogs, tongues hanging over their lips, guarded the front entrance. The little old craftsman, who had not spoken since he had left his workshop, remained mystified by the purpose of the journey until the minister turned to him and offered:

"A small, inadequate gift and my feeble attempt to repay you in kind."

The craftsman fell to his knees and begged forgiveness of the mandarin as he knew it was forbidden for an artisan to accept gifts from a foreigner. The mandarin raised the frightened blue figure from the ground, explaining to his countryman that the Empress herself had sanctioned the minister's request. A smile of joy came over the face of the craftsman and he slowly walked up to the doorway of the beautiful little house, unable to resist running his hand over the carved lion-dogs. The three travelers then spent more than an hour admiring the little house before returning in silent mutual happiness back to the workshop in Ha Li Chuan. The craftsman and the minister parted, honor satisfied, and Sir Alexander rode to his Embassy that night content that his actions had met with the approval of the mandarin as well as Lady Heathcote.

The minister completed his tour of duty in Peking, and the Empress awarded him the Silver Star of China and a grateful Queen added the K.C.V.O. to his already long list of decorations. After a few weeks back at the Foreign Office clearing the China desk, Sir Alexander retired to his native Yorkshire, the only English county whose inhabitants still hope to be born and die in the same place—not unlike the Chinese. Sir Alexander spent his final years in the home of his late father with his wife and the little Ming Emperor. The statue occupied the center of the mantelpiece in the drawing room for all to see and admire.

Being an exact man, Sir Alexander wrote a long and detailed will, in which he left precise instructions for the disposal of his estate, including what was to happen to the little statue after his death. He bequeathed the Emperor

Kung to his first son, requesting that he do the same, in order that the statue might always pass to the first son, or a daughter if the direct male line faltered. He also made a provision that the statue was never to be disposed of, unless the family's honor was at stake. Sir Alexander Heathcote died at the stroke of midnight on his seventieth year.

His firstborn, Major James Heathcote, was serving his Queen in the Boer War at the time he came into possession of the Ming Emperor. The colonel was a fighting man, commissioned with the Duke of Wellington's Regiment, and although he had little interest in culture, even he could see that the family heirloom was no ordinary treasure, so he loaned the statue to the regimental mess at Halifax in order that the Emperor could be displayed in the dining room for his brother officers to appreciate.

When James Heathcote became Colonel of the Dukes, the Emperor stood proudly on the table alongside the trophies won at Waterloo and Sebastopol in the Crimea and Madrid. And there the Ming statue remained until the colonel's retirement to his father's house in Yorkshire, when the Emperor returned once again to the drawing room mantelpiece. The colonel was not a man to disobey his late father, even in death, and he left clear instructions that the heirloom must always be passed on to the firstborn of the Heathcotes unless the family honor was in jeopardy. Colonel James Heathcote M.C. did not die a soldier's death; he simply fell asleep one night by the fire, the *Yorkshire Post* on his lap.

The colonel's firstborn, the Reverend Alexander Heathcote, was at the time presiding over a small flock in the parish of Honiton in Devon. After burying his father with military honors, he placed the little Ming Emperor on the mantelpiece of the vicarage. Few members of the Mothers' Union appreciated the masterpiece, but one or two old ladies were heard to remark on its delicate carving. And it was not until the Reverend became the Right Reverend, and the little statue found its way into the Bishop's Palace, that the Emperor attracted the admiration he deserved. Many of those who visited the palace and heard the story of how the Bishop's grandfather had acquired the Ming statue were fascinated to learn of the disparity between the magnificent statue and its base. It always made a good after-dinner story.

God takes even his own ambassadors, but He did not do so before allowing Bishop Heathcote to complete a will leaving the statue to his son, with his grandfather's exact instructions carefully repeated. The Bishop's son, Captain James Heathcote, was a serving officer in his grandfather's regiment, so the Ming statue returned to the mess table in Halifax. During the Emperor's absence, the regimental trophies had been augmented by those struck for Ypres, the Marne and Verdun. The regiment was once again at war with Germany, and young Captain James Heathcote was killed on the beaches of Dunkirk and died intestate. Thereafter, English law, the known wishes of his great-grandfather and common sense prevailed and the little Emperor came into the possession of the captain's two-year-old son.

Alex Heathcote was, alas, not of the mettle of his doughty ancestors and he grew up feeling no desire to serve anyone other than himself. When Captain James had been so tragically killed, Alexander's mother lavished everything on the boy that her meager income would allow. It didn't help, and it was not entirely young Alex's fault that he grew up to be, in the words of his grandmother, a selfish, spoiled little brat.

When Alex left school, only a short time before he would have been expelled, he found he could never hold down a job for more than a few weeks. It always seemed necessary for him to spend a little more than he, and finally his mother, could cope with. The good lady, deciding she could take no more of this life, departed it, to join all the other Heathcotes, not in Yorkshire, but in heaven.

In the swinging sixties, when casinos opened in Britain, young Alex was convinced that he had found the ideal way of earning a living without actually having to do any work. He developed a system for playing roulette with which it was impossible to lose. He did lose, so he refined the system and promptly lost more; he refined the system once again, which forced him to borrow to cover his losses. Why not? If the worst came to the worst, he reassured himself, he could always dispose of the little Ming Emperor.

The worst did come to the worst as each one of Alex's newly refined systems took him progressively into greater debt until the casinos began to press him for payment. When finally, one Monday morning, Alex received an unsolicited call from two gentlemen who seemed determined to collect some eight thousand pounds he owed their masters, and hinted at bodily harm if the matter was not dealt with within fourteen days, Alex caved in. After all, his great-great-grandfather's instructions had been exact: the Ming statue was to be sold if the family honor was ever at stake.

Alex took the little Emperor off the mantelpiece in his Cadogan Gardens flat and stared down at its delicate handiwork, at least having the grace to feel a little sad at the loss of the family heirloom. He then drove to Bond Street and delivered the masterpiece to Sotheby's, giving instructions for the Emperor to be put up for auction.

The head of the Oriental department, a pale, thin man, appeared at the front desk to discuss the masterpiece with Alex, looking not unlike the Ming statue he was holding so lovingly in his hands.

"It will take a few days to estimate the true value of the piece," he purred, "but I feel confident on a cursory glance that the statue is as fine an example of Pen Q as we have ever had under the hammer."

"That's no problem," replied Alex, "as long as you can let me know what it's worth within fourteen days."

"Oh, certainly," replied the expert. "I feel sure I could give you a floor price by Friday."

"Couldn't be better," said Alex.

During that week he contacted all his creditors and without exception they were prepared to wait and learn the appraisal of the expert. Alex duly returned to Bond Street on the Friday with a large smile on his face. He knew what his great-great-grandfather had paid for the piece and felt confident that the statue must be worth more than ten thousand pounds. A sum that would not only yield him enough to cover all his debts but leave him a little over to try out his new refined, refined system on the roulette table. As he climbed the steps of Sotheby's, Alex silently thanked his great-great-grandfather. He asked the girl on reception if he could speak to the head of the Oriental department. She picked up an internal phone, and the expert appeared a few moments later at the front desk with a somber look on his face. Alex's heart sank as he listened to his words:

"A nice little piece, your Emperor, but unfortunately a fake, probably about two hundred, two hundred and fifty years old but only a copy of the original, I'm afraid. Copies were often made because . . ."

"How much is it worth?" interrupted an anxious Alex.

"Seven hundred pounds, eight hundred at the most."

Enough to buy a gun and some bullets, thought Alex sardonically as he turned and started to walk away.

"I wonder, sir . . ." continued the expert.

"Yes, yes, sell the bloody thing," said Alex, without bothering to look back.

"And what do you want me to do with the base?"

"The base?" repeated Alex, turning round to face the Orientalist.

"Yes, the base. It's quite magnificent, fifteenth century, undoubtedly a work of genius, I can't imagine how . . ."

"Lot Number 103," announced the auctioneer. "What am I bid for this magnificent example of . . .?"

The expert turned out to be right in his assessment. At the auction at Sotheby's that Thursday morning I obtained the little Emperor for seven hundred and twenty guineas. And the base? That was acquired by an American gentleman of not unknown parentage for twenty-two thousand guineas.

The Luncheon

SHE WAVED TO ME across a crowded room at the St. Regis Hotel in New York. I waved back, realizing I knew the face, but I was unable to place it. She squeezed past waiters and guests and had reached me before I had a chance to ask anyone who she was. I racked that section of my brain which is meant to store people, but it transmitted no reply. I realized I would have to resort to the old party trick of carefully worded questions until her answers jogged my memory.

"How *are* you, darling?" she cried, and threw her arms around me, an opening that didn't help as we were at a Literary Guild cocktail party, and anyone will throw their arms around you on such occasions, even the directors of the Book-of-the-Month Club. From her accent she was clearly American and looked to be approaching forty but, thanks to the genius of modern makeup, might even have overtaken it. She wore a long white cocktail dress and her blond hair was done up in one of those buns that look like a cottage loaf. The overall effect made her appear somewhat like a chess queen. Not that the cottage loaf helped, because she might have had dark hair flowing to her shoulders when we last met. I do wish women would realize that when they change their hair style they often achieve exactly what they set out to do—look completely different to any unsuspecting male.

"I'm well, thank you," I said to the white queen. "And you?" I inquired as my opening gambit.

"I'm just fine, darling," she replied, taking a glass of champagne from a passing waiter.

"And how's the family?" I asked, not sure if she even had one.

"They're all well," she replied. No help there. "And how is Louise?" she inquired.

"Blooming," I said. So she knew my wife. But then not necessarily, I thought. Most American women are experts at remembering the names of men's wives. They have to be, since on the New York circuit they change so often it becomes a greater challenge than *The Times* crossword.

"Have you been to London lately?" I roared above the babble. A brave question, as she might never have been to Europe.

"Only once since we had lunch together." She looked at me quizzically. "You don't remember who I am, do you?" she asked as she devoured a cocktail sausage.

I smiled.

"Don't be silly, Susan," I said. "How could I ever forget?"

She smiled.

I confess that I remembered the white queen's name in the nick of time. Although I still had only vague recollections of the lady, I certainly would never forget the lunch.

I had just had my first book published and the critics on both sides of the Atlantic had been complimentary, even if the checks from my publishers were less so. My agent had told me on several occasions that I shouldn't write if I wanted to make money. This created a dilemma because I couldn't see how to make money if I didn't write.

It was around this time that the lady, who was now facing me and chattering on oblivious to my silence, telephoned from New York to heap lavish praise on my novel. There is no writer who does not enjoy receiving such calls, although I confess to having been less than captivated by an eleven-year-old girl who called me collect from California to say she had found a spelling mistake on page forty-seven and warned me she would ring again if she discovered another. However, this particular lady might have ended her transatlantic congratulations with nothing more than goodbye if she had not dropped her own name. It was one of those names that can, on the spur of the moment, always book a table at a chic restaurant or a seat at the opera which mere mortals like myself would have found impossible to achieve given a month's notice. To be fair, it was her husband's name that had achieved the reputation, as one of the world's most distinguished film producers.

"When I'm next in London you must have lunch with me," came crackling down the phone.

"No," said I gallantly, "you must have lunch with *me*."

"How perfectly charming you English always are," she said.

I have often wondered how much American women get away with when they say those few words to an Englishman. Nevertheless, the wife of an Oscar-winning producer does not phone one every day.

"I promise to call you when I'm next in London," she said.

And indeed she did; almost six months to the day she telephoned again, this time from the Connaught Hotel to declare how much she was looking forward to our meeting.

"Where would you like to have lunch?" I said, realizing a second too late, when she replied with the name of one of the most exclusive restaurants in town, that I should have made sure it was I who chose the venue. I was glad she couldn't see my forlorn face as she added with unabashed liberation:

"Monday, one o'clock. Leave the booking to me—I'm known there."

On the day in question I donned my one respectable suit, a new shirt which I had been saving for a special occasion since Christmas, and the only tie that looked as if it hadn't previously been used to hold up my trousers. I then strolled over to my bank and asked for a statement of my current account. The teller handed me a long piece of paper unworthy of its amount. I studied the figure as one who has to take a major financial decision. The bottom line stated in black lettering that I had a total balance of thirty-seven pounds and sixty-three pence. I wrote out a check for thirty-seven pounds. I feel that a gentleman should always leave his account in credit, and I might add it was a belief that my bank manager shared with me. I then walked up to Mayfair for my luncheon date.

As I entered the restaurant I observed too many waiters and plush seats for my liking. You can't eat either, but you can be charged for them. At a corner table for two sat a woman who, although not young, was elegant. She wore a blouse of powder blue crepe de Chine, and her blond hair was rolled away from her face in a style that reminded me of the war years and had once again become fashionable. It was clearly my transatlantic admirer and she greeted me in the same "I've known you all my life" fashion as she was to do at the Literary Guild cocktail party years later. Although she had a drink in front of her I didn't order an apéritif, explaining that I never drank before lunch—and would like to have added, "But as soon as your husband makes a film of my novel, I will."

She launched immediately into the latest Hollywood gossip, not so much dropping names as reciting them, while I ate my way through the crisps from the bowl in front of me. A few minutes later a waiter materialized by the table and presented us with two large embossed leather menus, considerably better bound than my novel. The place positively reeked of unnecessary expense. I opened the menu and studied the first chapter with horror; it was eminently put-downable. I had no idea that simple food obtained from Covent Garden that morning could cost quite so much by merely being transported to Mayfair. I could have bought her the same dishes for a quarter of the price at my favorite bistro, a mere one hundred yards away, and to add to my discomfort I observed that it was one of those restaurants where the guest's menu made no mention of the prices. I settled down to study the long list of French dishes, which only served to remind me that I hadn't eaten well for over a month, a state of affairs that was about to be prolonged by a further day. I remembered my bank balance and morosely reflected that I would probably have to wait until my agent sold the Icelandic rights of my novel before I could afford a square meal again.

"What would you like?" I said gallantly.

"I always enjoy a light lunch," she volunteered. I sighed with premature relief, only to find that light did not necessarily mean "inexpensive."

She smiled sweetly up at the waiter, who looked as if *he* wouldn't be wondering where his next meal would be coming from, and ordered just a sliver of smoked salmon, followed by two tiny tender lamb cutlets. Then she hesitated, but only for a moment, before adding, "And a side salad."

I studied the menu with some caution, running my finger down the prices, not the dishes.

"I also eat lightly at lunch," I said mendaciously. "The

chef's salad will be quite enough for me." The waiter was obviously affronted but left peaceably.

She chatted of Coppola and Preminger, of Al Pacino and Robert Redford, and of Greta Garbo as if she saw her all the time. She was kind enough to stop for a moment and ask what I was working on at present. I would have liked to reply something about how was I going to explain to my wife that I only had sixty-three pence left in our joint account, but I actually discussed my ideas for another novel. She seemed impressed but still made no reference to her husband. Should I mention him? No. Mustn't sound pushy, or as though I needed the money.

The food arrived, or that is to say her smoked salmon did, and I sat silently watching her eat my bank account while I nibbled a roll. I looked up only to discover a wine waiter hovering by my side.

"Would you care for some wine?" said I, recklessly.

"No, I don't think so," she said. I smiled a little too soon: "Well, perhaps a little something white and dry."

The wine waiter handed over a second leather-bound book, this time with golden grapes embossed on the cover. I searched down the pages for half bottles, explaining to my guest that I never drank at lunch. I chose the cheapest. The wine waiter reappeared a moment later with a large silver salver full of ice in which the half bottle looked drowned, and, like me, completely out of its depth. A junior waiter cleared away the empty plate while another wheeled a large trolley to the side of our table and served the lamb cutlets and the chef's salad. At the same time a third waiter made up an exquisite side salad for my guest which ended up bigger than my complete order. I didn't feel I could ask her to swap.

To be fair, the chef's salad was superb—although I confess it was hard to appreciate such food fully while trying to work out a plot that would be convincing if I found the bill came to more than thirty-seven pounds.

"How silly of me to ask for white wine with lamb," she said, having nearly finished the half bottle. I ordered a half bottle of the house red without calling for the wine list.

She finished the white wine and then launched into the theater, music and other authors. All those who were still alive she seemed to know and those who were dead she hadn't read. I might have enjoyed the performance if it hadn't been for the fear of wondering if I would be able to afford it when the curtain came down. When the waiter cleared away the empty dishes he asked my guest if she would care for anything else.

"No, thank you," she said—I nearly applauded. "Unless you have one of your famous apple surprises."

"I fear the last one may have gone, madam, but I'll go and check."

Don't hurry, I wanted to say, but instead I just smiled as the rope tightened around my neck. A few moments later the waiter strode back in triumph weaving between the tables holding the apple surprise in the palm of his hand, high above his head. I prayed to Newton that the apple would obey his law. It didn't.

"The last one, madam."

"Oh, what luck," she declared.

"Oh, what luck," I repeated, unable to face the menu and discover the price. I was now attempting some mental arithmetic as I realized it was going to be a close-run thing.

"Anything else, madam?" the ingratiating waiter inquired.

I took a deep breath.

"Just coffee," she said.

"And for you, sir?"

"No, no, not for me." He left us. I couldn't think of an explanation for why I didn't drink coffee.

She then produced from the large Gucci bag by her side

a copy of my novel, which I signed with a flourish, hoping the headwaiter would see me and feel I was the sort of man who should be allowed to sign the bill as well, but he resolutely remained at the far end of the room while I wrote the words "An unforgettable meeting" and appended my signature.

While the dear lady was drinking her coffee I picked at another roll and called for the bill, not because I was in any particular hurry, but like a guilty defendant at the Old Bailey I preferred to wait no longer for the judge's sentence. A man in a smart green uniform, whom I had never seen before, appeared carrying a silver tray with a folded piece of paper on it looking not unlike my bank statement. I pushed back the edge of the check slowly and read the figure: thirty-six pounds and forty pence. I casually put my hand into my inside pocket and withdrew my life's possessions and then placed the crisp new notes on the silver tray. They were whisked away. The man in the green uniform returned a few moments later with my sixty pence change, which I pocketed as it was the only way I was going to get a bus home. The waiter gave me a look that would have undoubtedly won him a character part in any film produced by the lady's distinguished husband.

My guest rose and walked across the restaurant, waving at and occasionally kissing people that I had previously only seen in glossy magazines. When she reached the door she stopped to retrieve her coat, a mink. I helped her on with the fur, again failing to leave a tip. As we stood on the Curzon Street pavement, a dark blue Rolls-Royce drew up beside us and a liveried chauffeur leaped out and opened the rear door. She climbed in.

"Goodbye, darling," she said, as the electric window slid down. "Thank you for such a lovely lunch."

"Goodbye," I said, and summoning up my courage added: "I do hope when you are next in town I shall have the opportunity of meeting your distinguished husband."

"Oh, darling, didn't you know?" she said as she looked out from the Rolls-Royce.

"Know what?"

"We were divorced ages ago."

"Divorced?" said I.

"Oh, yes," she said gaily, "I haven't spoken to him for years."

I just stood there looking helpless.

"Oh, don't worry yourself on my account," she said. "He's no loss. In any case, I have recently married again"—another film producer, I prayed—"in fact, I quite expected to bump into my husband today: you see, he owns the restaurant."

Without another word the electric window purred up and the Rolls-Royce glided effortlessly out of sight, leaving me to walk to the nearest bus stop.

As I stood surrounded by Literary Guild guests, staring at the white queen with the cottage loaf bun, I could still see her drifting away in that blue Rolls-Royce. I tried to concentrate on her words.

"I knew you wouldn't forget me, darling," she was saying. "After all, I did take you to lunch, didn't I?"

The Coup

THE BLUE AND SILVER 707 JET, displaying a large "P" on its tail plane, taxied to a halt at the north end of Lagos International Airport. A fleet of six black Mercedes drove up to the side of the aircraft and waited in a line resembling a land-bound crocodile. Six sweating uniformed drivers leaped out and stood to attention. When the driver of the front car opened his rear door, Colonel Usman of the Federal Guard stepped out and walked quickly to the bottom of the passenger steps, which had been hurriedly pushed into place by four of the airport staff.

The cabin door of the front section swung back and the colonel stared up into the gap, to see, framed against the dark interior of the cabin, a slim, attractive hostess dressed in a blue suit with silver piping. On her jacket lapel was a large "P." She turned and nodded in the direction of the cabin. A few seconds later, a tall, immaculately dressed man with thick black hair and deep-brown eyes replaced her in the doorway. The man had about him an air of effortless style which self-made millionaires would have paid a considerable part of their fortune to possess. The colonel saluted as Senhor Eduardo Francisco de Silveira, head of the Prentino empire, nodded curtly.

De Silveira emerged from the coolness of his air-conditioned 707 into the burning Nigerian sun without showing the slightest sign of discomfort. The colonel guided the tall, elegant Brazilian, who was accompanied only by his private secretary, to the front Mercedes while the rest of the Prentino staff filed down the back stairway of the aircraft and filled the other five cars. The driver, a corporal who had been detailed to be available night and day for the honored guest, opened the rear door of the front car and saluted. Eduardo de Silveira showed no sign of acknowledgment. The corporal smiled nervously, revealing the largest set of white teeth the Brazilian had ever seen.

"Welcome to Lagos," the corporal volunteered. "Hope you make very big deal while you are in Nigeria."

Eduardo did not comment as he settled back into his seat and stared out of the tinted window to watch some passengers of a British Airways 707 that had landed just before him form a long queue on the hot tarmac as they waited patiently to clear customs. The driver put the car into first gear and the black crocodile proceeded on its journey. Colonel Usman, who was now in the front seat beside the corporal, soon discovered that the Brazilian guest did not care for small talk, and the secretary who was seated by his employer's side never once opened his mouth. The colonel, used to doing things by example, remained silent, leaving de Silveira to consider his plan of campaign.

Eduardo Francisco de Silveira had been born in the small village of Rebeti, a hundred miles north of Rio de Janeiro, heir to one of the two most powerful family fortunes in Brazil. He had been educated privately in Switzerland before attending the University of California in Los Angeles. He went on to complete his education at the Harvard Business School. After Harvard he returned from America to work in Brazil, where he started neither at the top nor at the bottom of the firm but in the middle, managing his family's mining interests in Minas Gerais. He quickly worked his way to the top, even faster than his father had planned, but then the boy turned out to be not so much a chip as a chunk off the old block. At twenty-nine he married Maria, eldest daughter of his father's closest friend, and when twelve years later his father died Eduardo succeeded to the Prentino throne. There were seven sons in all: the second son, Alfredo, was now in charge of banking; João ran shipping; Carlos organized construction; Manoel arranged food and supplies; Jaime managed the family newspapers; and little Antonio, the last—and certainly the least—ran the family farms. All the brothers reported to Eduardo before making any major decision, for he was still chairman of the largest private company in Brazil, despite the boastful claims of his old family enemy, Manuel Rodriguez.

When General Castelo Branco's military regime overthrew the civilian government in 1964 the generals agreed that they could not kill off all the de Silveiras or the Rodriguezes so they had better learn to live with the two rival families. The de Silveiras for their part had always had enough sense never to involve themselves in politics other than by making payments to every government official, military or civilian, according to his rank. This ensured that the Prentino empire grew alongside whatever faction came to power. One of the reasons Eduardo de Silveira had allocated four days in his crowded schedule for a visit to Lagos was that the Nigerian system of government seemed to resemble so closely that of Brazil, and at least on this project he had cut the ground from under Manuel Rodriguez's feet, which would more than make up for losing the Rio airport tender to him. Eduardo smiled at the thought of Rodriguez's not realizing that he was in

Nigeria to close a deal that could make him twice the size of his rival.

As the black Mercedes moved slowly through the teeming, noisy streets paying no attention to traffic lights, red or green, Eduardo thought back to his first meeting with General Mohammed, the Nigerian Head of State, on the occasion of the President's official visit to Brazil. Speaking at the dinner given in General Mohammed's honor, President Ernesto Geisel declared a hope that the two countries would move toward closer cooperation in politics and commerce. Eduardo agreed with his unelected leader and was happy to leave the politics to the President if he allowed him to get on with the commerce. General Mohammed made his reply, on behalf of the guests, in an English accent that normally would be associated with Oxford. The General talked at length of the project that was most dear to his heart, the building of a new Nigerian capital in Abuja, a city that he hoped might even rival Brasilia. After the speeches were over, the General took de Silveira to one side and spoke in greater detail of the Abuja city project, asking him if he might consider a private tender. Eduardo smiled and only wished that his enemy, Rodriguez, could hear the intimate conversation he was having with the Nigerian Head of State.

Eduardo carefully studied the outline proposal sent to him a week later, after the General had returned to Nigeria, and agreed to his first request by dispatching a research team of seven men to fly to Lagos and complete a feasibility study on Abuja.

One month later, the team's detailed report was in de Silveira's hands. Eduardo came to the conclusion that the potential profitability of the project was worthy of a full proposal to the Nigerian government. He contacted General Mohammed personally to find that he was in full agreement and authorized the go-ahead. This time twenty-three men were dispatched to Lagos and three months and 170 pages later, Eduardo signed and sealed the proposal designated as "A New Capital for Nigeria." He made only one alteration to the final document. The cover of the proposal was in blue and silver with the Prentino logo in the center: Eduardo had that changed to green and white, the national colors of Nigeria, with the national emblem of an eagle astride two horses: he realized it was the little things that impressed generals and often tipped the scales. He sent ten copies of the feasibility study to Nigeria's Head of State with an invoice for one million dollars.

When General Mohammed had studied the proposal he invited Eduardo de Silveira to visit Nigeria as his guest, in order to discuss the next stage of the project. De Silveira telexed back, provisionally accepting the invitation and pointing out politely but firmly that he had not yet received reimbursement for the one million dollars spent on the initial feasibility study. The money was telexed by return from the Central Bank of Nigeria, and de Silveira managed to find four consecutive days in his calendar for "The New Federal Capital Project": his schedule demanded that he arrive in Lagos on a Monday morning because he had to be in Paris by Thursday night at the latest.

While these thoughts were going through Eduardo's mind, the Mercedes drew up outside Dodan Barracks. The iron gates swung open and a full armed guard gave the general salute, an honor normally afforded only to a visiting Head of State. The black Mercedes drove slowly through the gates and came to a halt outside the President's private residence. A brigadier waited on the steps to escort de Silveira through to the President.

The two men had lunch together in a small room that closely resembled a British officers' mess. The meal consisted of a steak that would not have been acceptable to any South American cowhand, surrounded by vegetables that reminded Eduardo of his schooldays. Still, Eduardo had never yet met a soldier who understood that a good chef was every bit as important as a good batman. During the lunch they talked in overall terms about the problems of building a whole new city in the middle of an equatorial jungle.

The provisional estimate of the cost of the project had been $1,000 million, but when de Silveira warned the President that the final outcome might well end up nearer $3,000 million, the President's jaw dropped slightly. De Silveira had to admit that the project would be the most ambitious that Prentino International had ever tackled, but he was quick to point out to the President that the same would be true of any construction company in the world.

De Silveira, not a man to play his best card early, waited until the coffee to slip into the conversation the fact that he had just been awarded, against heavy opposition (which had included Rodriguez), the contract to build an eight-lane highway through the Amazonian jungle, which would eventually link up with the Pan-American highway, a contract second in size only to the one they were now contemplating in Nigeria. The President was impressed and inquired if the venture would not prevent de Silveira from involving himself in the new capital project.

"I'll know the answer to that question in three days' time," replied the Brazilian, and agreed to a further discussion with the Head of State at the end of his visit, when he would let the President know if he was prepared to continue with the scheme.

After lunch Eduardo was driven to the Federal Palace Hotel, where the entire sixth floor had been placed at his disposal. Several complaining guests who had come to Nigeria to close deals involving mere millions had been asked to vacate their rooms at short notice to make way for de Silveira and his staff. Eduardo knew nothing of these goings-on, as there was always a room available for him wherever he arrived in the world.

The six Mercedes drew up outside the hotel, and the colonel guided his charge through the swing doors and past reception. Eduardo had not checked himself into a hotel for the past fourteen years except on those occasions when he chose to register under an assumed name, not wanting anyone to know the identity of the woman he was with.

The chairman of Prentino International walked down the center of the hotel's main corridor and stepped into a waiting lift. His legs went weak and he suddenly felt sick. In the corner of the lift stood a stubby, balding, overweight man, who was dressed in a pair of old jeans and a T-shirt, his mouth continually opening and closing as he chewed gum. The two men stood as far apart as possible, neither showing any sign of recognition. The lift stopped at the fifth floor and Manuel Rodriguez, chairman of Rodriguez International S.A., stepped out, leaving behind him the man who had been his bitter rival for thirty years.

Eduardo held on to the rail in the lift to steady himself because he still felt dizzy. How he despised that uneducated self-made upstart whose family of four half-brothers, all by different fathers, claimed they now ran the largest construction company in Brazil. Both men were as interested in the other's failure as they were in their own success.

Eduardo was somewhat puzzled to know what Rodriguez could possibly be doing in Lagos for he felt certain that his rival had not come into contact with the Nigerian President. After all, Eduardo had never collected the rent on a small house in Rio that was occupied by the mistress of a very senior official in the government's protocol department. And the man's only task was to be certain that Rodriguez was not invited to any function attended by a visiting dignitary when in Brazil. The continual absence of Rodriguez from these state occasions ensured the absent-mindedness of Eduardo's rent collector in Rio.

Eduardo would never have admitted to anyone that Rodriguez' presence worried him, but he nevertheless resolved to find out immediately what had brought his old enemy to Nigeria. Once he reached his suite de Silveira instructed his private secretary to check what Manuel Rodriguez was up to. Eduardo was prepared to fly on to Paris immediately if Rodriguez turned out to be involved in any way with the new capital project, and one young lady in Rio would suddenly find herself looking for other accommodations.

Within an hour his private secretary returned with the information his chairman had requested. Rodriguez, he had discovered, was in Nigeria to tender for the contract to construct a new port in Lagos and was apparently not involved in any way with the new capital, and in fact was still trying to arrange a meeting with the President.

"Which minister is in charge of the ports and when am I due to see him?" asked de Silveira.

The secretary delved into his appointments file. "The Minister of Transport," the secretary said. "You have an appointment with him at nine o'clock on Thursday morning." The Nigerian Civil Service had mapped out a four-day schedule of meetings for de Silveira which included every cabinet minister involved in the new city project. "It's the last meeting before your final discussion with the President. You then fly on to Paris."

"Excellent. Remind me of this conversation five minutes before I see the minister and again when I talk to the President."

The secretary made a note in the file and left.

Eduardo sat alone in his suite, going over the reports

on the new capital project submitted by his experts. Some of his team were already showing signs of nervousness. One particular anxiety that always came up with a large construction contract was the principal's ability to pay, and pay on time. Failure to be paid on time was the quickest route to bankruptcy, but since the discovery of oil in Nigeria, there seemed to be no shortage of income and certainly no shortage of people willing to spend that money on behalf of the government. These anxieties did not worry de Silveira, because he always insisted on a substantial payment in advance; otherwise he wouldn't move himself or his vast staff one centimeter out of Brazil. However, the massive scope of this particular contract made the circumstances somewhat unusual. Eduardo realized that it would be most damaging to his international reputation if he started the assignment and then was seen not to complete it. He re-read the reports over a quiet dinner in his room and retired to bed early, having wasted an hour in vainly trying to place a call through to his wife.

De Silveira's first appointment the next morning was with the Governor of the Central Bank of Nigeria. Eduardo wore a newly pressed suit, fresh shirt and highly polished shoes: for four days no one would see him in the same clothes. At eight forty-five there was a quiet knock on the door of his suite and the secretary opened it to find Colonel Usman standing to attention, waiting to escort Eduardo to the bank. As they were leaving the hotel Eduardo again saw Manuel Rodriguez, wearing the same pair of jeans, the same crumpled T-shirt, and probably chewing the same gum as he stepped into a BMW in front of him. De Silveira stopped scowling at the disappearing BMW only when he remembered his Thursday morning appointment with the Minister of Transport, followed by a meeting with the President.

The Governor of the Central Bank of Nigeria was in

the habit of proposing how payment schedules would be met and completion orders would be guaranteed. He had never been told by anyone that if the payment was seven days overdue he could consider the contract null and void and that he could take it or leave it. The Governor would have made some comment if Abuja had not been the President's pet project. That position established, de Silveira went on to check the bank's reserves, long-term deposits, overseas commitments and estimated oil revenues for the next five years. He left the Governor in what could only be described as a jelly-like state, glistening and wobbling.

Eduardo's next appointment was an unavoidable courtesy call on the Brazilian Ambassador for lunch. He hated such functions, for he believed embassies to be fit only for cocktail parties and discussion of out-of-date trivia, neither of which he cared for. The food in such establishments was invariably bad and the company worse. It turned out to be no different on this occasion and the only profit (Eduardo considered everything in terms of profit and loss) to be derived from the encounter was the information that Manuel Rodriguez was on a short list of three for the building of the new port in Lagos and was expecting to have an audience with the President on Friday if he was awarded the contract. By Thursday morning that will be a short list of two and there will be no meeting with the President, de Silveira promised himself, and decided that that was the most he was likely to gain from the lunch—until the Ambassador added:

"Rodriguez seems most keen on seeing you awarded the new city contract at Abuja. He's singing your praises to every minister he meets. Funny," the Ambassador continued, "I always thought you two didn't see eye to eye."

Eduardo made no reply as he tried to fathom what trick Rodriguez could be up to by promoting his cause.

Eduardo spent the afternoon with the Minister of Finance

and confirmed the provisional arrangements he had made with the Governor of the bank. The Minister of Finance had been forewarned by the Governor what he was to expect from an encounter with Eduardo de Silveira and that he was not to be taken aback by the Brazilian's curt demands. De Silveira, aware that this warning would have taken place, let the poor man bargain a little and even gave way on a few minor points that he would be able to tell the President about at the next meeting of the Supreme Military Council. Eduardo left the smiling minister believing that he had scored a point or two against the formidable South American.

That evening, Eduardo dined privately with his senior advisers, who themselves were already dealing with the ministers' officials. Each was now coming up with daily reports about the problems that would have to be faced if they worked in Nigeria. His chief engineer was quick to emphasize that skilled labor could not be hired at any price, because the Germans had already cornered the market for their extensive road projects. The financial advisers also presented a gloomy report, of international companies waiting six months or more for their checks to be cleared by the central bank. Eduardo made notes on the views they expressed but never ventured an opinion himself. His staff left him a little after eleven and he decided to take a stroll around the hotel grounds before retiring to bed. On his walk through the luxuriant tropical gardens he only just avoided a face-to-face confrontation with Manuel Rodriguez by darting behind a large Iroko plant. The little man passed by champing away at his gum, oblivious to Eduardo's baleful glare. Eduardo informed a chattering gray parrot of his most secret thoughts: By Thursday afternoon, Rodriguez, you will be on your way back to Brazil with a suitcase full of plans that can be filed under "abortive projects." The parrot cocked its head and screeched at Eduardo as if it had been let in on his secret. Eduardo allowed himself a smile and returned to his room.

Colonel Usman arrived on the dot of eight forty-five again the next day and Eduardo spent the morning with the Minister of Supplies and Cooperatives—or lack of them, as he commented afterward to his private secretary. The afternoon was spent with the Minister of Labor checking over the availability of unskilled workers and the total lack of skilled operatives. Eduardo was fast reaching the conclusion that despite the professed optimism of the ministers concerned, this was going to be the toughest contract he had ever tackled. There was more to be lost than money if the whole international business world stood watching him fall flat on his face. In the evening his staff reported to him once again, having solved a few old problems and unearthed some new ones. Tentatively, they had come to the conclusion that if the present regime stayed in power, there need be no serious concern over payment, as the President had earmarked the new city as a priority project. They had even heard a rumor that the army would be willing to lend-lease part of the Service Corps if there turned out to be a shortage of skilled labor. Eduardo made a note to have this point confirmed in writing by the Head of State during their final meeting the next day. But the labor problem was not what was occupying Eduardo's thoughts as he put on his silk pajamas that night. He was chuckling at the idea of Manuel Rodriguez's imminent and sudden departure for Brazil. Eduardo slept well.

He rose with renewed vigor the next morning, showered and put on a fresh suit. The four days were turning out to be well worth while and a single stone might yet kill two birds. By eight forty-five he was waiting impatiently for the previously punctual colonel. The colonel did not show up at eight forty-five and had still not appeared when the clock on his mantelpiece struck nine. De Silveira sent his private secretary off to find out where he was and paced angrily backward and forward through the hotel suite. His secretary returned a few minutes later in a state of panic with the information that the hotel was surrounded by armed guards. Eduardo did not panic. He had been through eight coups in his life from which he had learned one golden rule: The new regime never kills visiting foreigners, because it needs their money every bit as much as the last government. Eduardo picked up the telephone, but no one answered so he switched on the radio. A tape recording was playing:

"This is Radio Nigeria, this is Radio Nigeria. There has been a coup. General Mohammed has been overthrown and Lieutenant Colonel Dimka has assumed leadership of the new revolutionary government. Do not be afraid; remain at home and everything will be back to normal in a few hours. This is Radio Nigeria, this is Radio Nigeria. There has been a . . ."

Eduardo switched off the radio as two thoughts flashed through his mind. Coups always held up everything and caused chaos, so undoubtedly he had wasted the four days. But worse, would it now be possible for him even to get out of Nigeria and carry on his normal business with the rest of the world?

By lunchtime the radio was playing martial music interspersed with the tape-recorded message he soon learned by heart. Eduardo detailed all his staff to find out anything they could and to report back to him direct. They all returned with the same story: that it was impossible to get past the soldiers surrounding the hotel, so no new information could be unearthed. Eduardo swore for the first time in months. To add to his inconvenience, the hotel manager rang through to say that regretfully Mr. de Silveira would have to eat in the main dining room as there would be no room service until further notice. Eduardo went down to the dining room somewhat reluctantly, only to discover that the headwaiter showed no interest in who he was and placed him unceremoniously at a small table already occupied by three Italians. Manuel Rodriguez was seated only two tables away: Eduardo stiffened at the thought of the other man enjoying his discomfiture and then remembered it was that morning he was supposed to have seen the Minister of Ports. He ate his meal quickly despite being served slowly and when the Italians tried to make conversation with him he waved them away with his hand, feigning lack of understanding, despite the fact that he spoke their language fluently. As soon as he had finished the second course he returned to his room. His staff had only gossip to pass on and they had been unable to make contact with the Brazilian Embassy to lodge an official protest. "A lot of good an official protest will do us," said Eduardo, slumping down in his chair. "Who do you send it to, the new regime or the old one?"

He sat alone in his room for the rest of the day, interrupted only by what he thought was the sound of gunfire in the distance. He read the New Federal Capital Project proposal and his advisers' reports for a third time.

The next morning Eduardo, dressed in the same suit as he had worn on the day of his arrival, was greeted by his secretary with the news that the coup had been crushed; after fierce street fighting, he informed his unusually attentive chairman, the old regime had regained power but not without losses; among those killed in the uprising had been General Mohammed, the Head of State. The secretary's news was officially confirmed on Radio Nigeria later that morning. The ringleader of the abortive coup, Lieutenant Colonel Dimka, along with one or two junior officers, had escaped, and the government had ordered a dusk-to-dawn curfew until the evil criminals were apprehended.

Pull off a coup and you're a national hero, fail and

you're an evil criminal; in business it's the same difference between bankruptcy and making a fortune, thought Eduardo as he listened to the news report. He was beginning to form plans in his mind for an early departure from Nigeria when the newscaster made an announcement that chilled him to the very marrow.

"While Lieutenant Colonel Dimka and his accomplices remain on the run, airports throughout the country will be closed until further notice."

When the newscaster had finished his report, martial music was played in memory of the late General Mohammed.

Eduardo went downstairs in a flaming temper. The hotel was still surrounded by armed guards. He stared at the fleet of six empty Mercedes which was parked only ten yards beyond the soldiers' rifles. He marched back into the foyer, irritated by the babble of different tongues coming at him from every direction. Eduardo looked around him: it was obvious that many people had been stranded in the hotel overnight and had ended up sleeping in the lounge or the bar. He checked the paperback rack in the lobby for something to read, but there were only four copies left of a tourist guide to Lagos; everything else had been sold. Authors who had not been read for years were now changing hands at a premium. Eduardo returned to his room, which was fast assuming the character of a prison, and balked at reading the New Federal Capital Project for a fourth time. He tried again to make contact with the Brazilian Ambassador to obtain special permission to leave the country since he had his own aircraft. No one answered the Embassy phone. He went down for an early lunch only to find that the dining room was once again packed to capacity. Eduardo was placed at a table with some Germans who were worrying about a contract that had been signed by the government the previous week, before the abortive coup. They were wondering if it would still be honored. Manuel Rodriguez entered the room a few minutes later and was placed at the next table.

During the afternoon, de Silveira ruefully examined his schedule for the next seven days. He had been due in Paris that morning to see the Minister of the Interior, and from there should have flown on to London to confer with the chairman of the Steel Board. His calendar was fully booked for the next ninety-two days until his family holiday in May. "I'm having this year's holiday in Nigeria," he commented wryly to an assistant.

What annoyed Eduardo most about the coup was the lack of communication it afforded with the outside world. He wondered what was going on in Brazil and he hated not being able to telephone or telex Paris or London to explain his absence personally. He listened addictively to Radio Nigeria on the hour every hour for any new scrap of information. At five o'clock he learned that the Supreme Military Council had elected a new President, who would address the nation on television and radio at nine o'clock that night.

Eduardo de Silveira switched on the television at eight forty-five; normally an assistant would have put it on for him at one minute to nine. He sat watching a Nigerian lady giving a talk on dressmaking, followed by the weather forecast man, who supplied Eduardo with the revealing information that the temperature would continue to be hot for the next month. Eduardo's knee was twitching up and down nervously as he waited for the address by the new President. At nine o'clock, after the national anthem had been played, the new Head of State, General Obasanjo, appeared on the screen in full dress uniform. He spoke first of the tragic death and sad loss for the nation of the late President and went on to say that his government would continue to work in the best interest of Nigeria. He looked ill at ease as he apologized to all foreign visitors who were inconvenienced by the attempted coup but went on to make it clear that the dusk-to-dawn curfew would continue until the rebel leaders were tracked down and brought to justice. He confirmed that all airports would remain closed until Lieutenant Colonel Dimka was in custody. The new President ended his statement by saying that all other forms of communication would be opened up again as soon as possible. The national anthem was played for a second time, as Eduardo thought of the millions of dollars that might be lost to him by his incarceration in that hotel room, while his private plane sat idly on the tarmac only a few miles away. One of his senior managers made book as to how long it would take for the authorities to capture Lieutenant Colonel Dimka; he did not tell de Silveira how short the odds were on a month.

Eduardo went down to the dining room in the suit he had worn the day before. A junior waiter placed him at a table with some Frenchmen who had been hoping to win a contract to drill for oil in the Niger state. Again Eduardo waved a languid hand when they tried to include him in their conversation. At that very moment he was meant to be with the French Minister of the Interior, not with some French oil drillers. He tried to concentrate on his watered-down soup, wondering how much longer it might be before it would be just water. The headwaiter appeared by his side, gesturing to the one remaining seat at the table, in which he placed Manuel Rodriguez. Still neither man gave any sign of recognizing the other. Eduardo debated with himself whether he should leave the table or carry on as if his oldest rival was still in Brazil. He decided the latter was more dignified. The Frenchmen began an argument among themselves as to when they would be able to get out of Lagos. One of them declared emphatically that he had heard on the highest authority that the government intended to track down every last one of those involved in the coup before they opened the airports and that might take up to a month.

"What?" said the two Brazilians together, in English.

"I can't hang around here for a month," said Eduardo.

"Neither can I," said Manuel Rodriguez.

"You'll have to, at least until Dimka is captured," said one of the Frenchmen, breaking into English. "So you must both relax yourselves, yes?"

The two Brazilians continued their meal in silence. When Eduardo had finished he rose from the table and without looking directly at Rodriguez said good night in Portuguese. The old rival inclined his head in reply.

The next day brought forth no new information. The hotel remained surrounded with soldiers and by the evening Eduardo had lost his temper with every member of his staff with whom he had come into contact. He went down to dinner on his own and as he entered the dining room he saw Manuel Rodriguez sitting alone at a table in the corner. Rodriguez looked up, seemed to hesitate for a moment, and then beckoned to Eduardo. Eduardo himself hesitated before walking slowly toward Rodriguez and taking the seat opposite him. Rodriguez poured him a glass of wine. Eduardo, who rarely drank, drank it. Their conversation was stilted to begin with, but as both men consumed more wine they each began to relax in the other's company. By the time coffee had arrived, Manuel was telling Eduardo what he could do with this godforsaken country.

"You will not stay on if you are awarded the ports contract?" inquired Eduardo.

"Not a hope," said Rodriguez, who showed no surprise that de Silveira knew of his interest in the ports contract. "I withdrew from the short list the day before the coup. I had intended to fly back to Brazil that Thursday morning."

"Can you say why you withdrew?"

"Labor problems mainly, and then the congestion of the ports."

"I am not sure I understand," said Eduardo, understanding full well but curious to learn if Rodriguez had picked up some tiny detail his own staff had missed.

Manuel Rodriguez paused to ingest the fact that the man he had viewed as his most dangerous enemy for over thirty years was now listening to his own inside information. He considered the situation for a moment while he sipped his coffee. Eduardo didn't speak.

"To begin with, there's a terrible shortage of skilled labor, and on top of that there's this mad quota system."

"Quota system?" said Eduardo innocently.

"The percentage of people from the contractor's country which the government will allow to work in Nigeria."

"Why should that be a problem?" said Eduardo, leaning forward.

"By law you have to employ at a ratio of fifty nationals to one foreigner, so I could only have brought over twenty-five of my top men to organize a fifty-million-dollar contract and I'd have had to make do with Nigerians at every other level. The government are cutting their own throats with the wretched system; they can't expect unskilled men, black or white, to become experienced engineers overnight. It's all to do with their national pride. Someone must tell them they can't afford that sort of pride if they want to complete the job at a sensible price. That path is the surest route to bankruptcy. On top of that, the Germans have already rounded up all the best skilled labor for their road projects."

"But surely," said Eduardo, "you charge according to the rules, however stupid, thus covering all eventualities, and as long as you're certain that payment is guaranteed . . ."

Manuel raised his hand to stop Eduardo's flow: "That's another problem. You can't be certain. The government reneged on a major steel contract only last month. In so doing," he explained, "they bankrupted a distinguished international company. So they are perfectly capable of trying the same trick with me. And if they don't pay up, who do you sue? The Supreme Military Council?"

"And the ports problem?"

"The port is totally congested. There are one hundred and seventy ships desperate to unload their cargo with a waiting time of anything up to six months. On top of that, there is a demurrage charge of five thousand dollars a day and only perishable foods are given any priority."

"But there's always a way round that sort of problem," said Eduardo, rubbing a thumb twice across the top of his fingers.

"Bribery? It doesn't work, Eduardo. How can you possibly jump the queue when all one hundred and seventy ships have already bribed the harbor master? And don't imagine that fixing the rent on a flat for one of his mistresses would help either," said Rodriguez, grinning. "With that man you will have to supply the mistress as well."

Eduardo held his breath but said nothing.

"Come to think of it," continued Rodriguez, "if the situation becomes any worse, the harbor master will be the one man in the country who is richer than you."

Eduardo laughed for the first time in three days.

"I tell you, Eduardo, we could make a bigger profit building a salt mine in Siberia."

Eduardo laughed again and some of the Prentino and Rodriguez staff dining at other tables stared in disbelief at their masters.

"You were in for the big one, the new city of Abuja?" said Manuel.

"That's right," admitted Eduardo.

"I have done everything in my power to make sure you were awarded that contract," said the other quietly.

"What?" said Eduardo in disbelief. "Why?"

"I thought Abuja would give the Prentino empire more headaches than even you could cope with, Eduardo, and that might possibly leave the field wide open for me at home. Think about it. Every time there's a cutback in Nigeria, what will be the first head to roll off the chopping block? 'The unnecessary city,' as the locals all call it."

"The unnecessary city?" repeated Eduardo.

"Yes, and it doesn't help when you say you won't move without advance payment. You know as well as I do, you will need one hundred of your best men here full time to organize such a massive enterprise. They'll need feeding, salaries, housing, perhaps even a school and a hospital. Once they are settled down here, you can't just pull them off the job every two weeks because the government is running late clearing the checks. It's not practical and you know it." Rodriguez poured Eduardo de Silveira another glass of wine.

"I had already taken that into consideration," Eduardo said as he sipped the wine, "but I thought that with the support of the Head of State . . ."

"The late Head of State—"

"I take your point, Manuel."

"Maybe the next Head of State will also back you, but what about the one after that? Nigeria has had three coups in the past three years."

Eduardo remained silent for a moment.

"Do you play backgammon?"

"Yes. Why do you ask?"

"I must make *some* money while I'm here."

Manuel laughed.

"Why don't you come to my room," continued de Silveira. "Though I must warn you I always manage to beat my staff."

"Perhaps they always manage to lose," said Manuel as he rose and grabbed the half-empty bottle of wine by its neck. Both men were laughing as they left the dining room.

After that, the two chairmen had lunch and dinner together every day. Within a week, their staff were eating at the same tables. Eduardo could be seen in the dining room without a tie while Manuel wore a shirt for the first time in years. By the end of a fortnight, the two rivals had played each other at table tennis, backgammon and bridge with the stakes set at one hundred dollars a point. At the end of each day Eduardo always seemed to end up owing Manuel about a million dollars, which Manuel happily traded for the best bottle of wine left in the hotel's cellar.

Although Lieutenant Colonel Dimka had been sighted by about forty thousand Nigerians in about as many different places, he still remained resolutely uncaptured. As the new President had insisted, airports remained closed, but communications were opened, which at least allowed Eduardo to telephone and telex Brazil. His brothers and wife were sending replies by the hour imploring Eduardo to return home at any cost: decisions on major contracts throughout the world were being held up by his absence. But Eduardo's message back to Brazil was always the same: as long as Dimka is on the loose, the airports will remain closed.

It was on a Tuesday night during dinner that Eduardo took the trouble to explain to Manuel why Brazil had lost the World Cup in soccer. Manuel dismissed Eduardo's outrageous claims as ill informed and prejudiced. It was the only subject on which they hadn't agreed in the past three weeks.

"I blame the whole fiasco on Zagalo," said Eduardo.

"No, no, you cannot blame the manager," said Manuel. "The fault lies with our stupid selectors who know even less about the sport than you do. They should never have dropped Leao from goal and in any case we should have learned from the Argentinian defeat last year that our methods are now out of date. You must attack, attack, if you want to score goals."

"Rubbish. We still have the surest defense in the world."

"Which means the best result you can hope for is a 0–0 draw."

"Never . . ." began Eduardo.

"Excuse me, sir."

Eduardo looked up to see his private secretary standing by his side looking anxiously down at him.

"Yes, what's the problem?"

"An urgent telex from Brazil, sir."

Eduardo read the first paragraph and then asked Manuel if he would be kind enough to excuse him for a few minutes. The latter nodded politely. Eduardo left the table and as he marched through the dining room seventeen other guests left unfinished meals and followed him quickly to his suite on the top floor, where the rest of his staff were already assembled. He sat down alone in the corner of the room. No one spoke as he read through the telex carefully, suddenly realizing how many days he had been imprisoned in Lagos.

The telex was from his brother Carlos and the contents concerned the Pan-American road project through the Amazonian jungle. Prentinos had tendered for the section that ran through the middle of the Amazon jungle and had to have the bank guarantees signed and certified by midday tomorrow, Tuesday. Eduardo had quite forgotten which Tuesday it was and the document he was committed to sign by the following day's deadline.

"What's the problem?" Eduardo asked his private secretary. "The Banco do Brasil have already agreed with Alfredo to act as guarantors. What's stopping Carlos from signing the agreement in my absence?"

"The Mexicans are now demanding that responsibility for the contract be shared because of the insurance problems: Lloyd's of London will not cover the entire risk if only one company is involved. The details are all on page seven of the telex."

Eduardo flicked quickly through the pages. He read that his brothers had already tried to put pressure on Lloyd's, but to no avail. That's like trying to bribe a maiden aunt into taking part in a public orgy, thought Eduardo, and he would have told them as much if he had been back in Brazil. The Mexican government was therefore insisting that the contract be shared with an international construction company acceptable to Lloyd's if the legal documents were to be signed by the midday deadline the following day.

"Stay put," said Eduardo to his staff, and he returned to the dining room alone, trailing the long telex behind him. Rodriguez watched him as he scurried back to their table.

"You look like a man with a problem."

"I am," said Eduardo. "Read that."

Manuel's experienced eye ran down the telex, picking out the salient points. He had tendered for the Amazon road project himself and could still recall the details. At Eduardo's insistence, he re-read page seven.

"Mexican bandits," he said as he returned the telex to Eduardo. "Who do they think they are, telling Eduardo de Silveira how he must conduct his business. Telex them back immediately and inform them you're chairman of the greatest construction company in the world and they can roast in hell before you will agree to their pathetic terms. You know it's far too late for them to go out to tender again with every other section of the highway ready to begin work. They would lose millions. Call their bluff, Eduardo."

"I think you may be right, Manuel, but any hold-up now can only waste my time and money, so I intend to agree to their demand and look for a partner."

"You'll never find one at such short notice."

"I will."

"Who?"

Eduardo de Silveira hesitated only for a second. "You, Manuel. I want to offer Rodriguez International S.A. fifty percent of the Amazon road contract."

Manuel Rodriguez looked up at Eduardo. It was the first time that he had not anticipated his old rival's next move. "I suppose it might help cover the millions you owe me in table tennis debts."

The two men laughed; then Rodriguez stood up and they shook hands gravely. De Silveira left the dining room on the run and wrote out a telex for his manager to transmit.

"Sign, accept terms, fifty percent partner will be Rodriguez International Construction S.A., Brazil."

"If I telex that message, sir, you do realize that it's legally binding?"

"Send it," said Eduardo.

Eduardo returned once again to the dining room, where Manuel had ordered the finest bottle of champagne in the hotel. Just as they were calling for a second bottle, and singing a spirited version of "*Esta Cheganda a hora,*" Eduardo's private secretary appeared by his side again, this time with two telexes, one from the President of the Banco do Brasil and a second from his brother Carlos. Both wanted confirmation of the agreed partner for the Amazon road project. Eduardo uncorked the second bottle of champagne without looking up at his private secretary.

"Confirm Rodriguez International Construction to the President of the bank and my brother," he said as he filled Manuel's empty glass. "And don't bother me again tonight."

"Yes, sir," said the private secretary, and left without another word.

Neither man could recall what time he climbed into bed that night, but de Silveira was abruptly awakened from a deep sleep by his secretary early the next morning. Eduardo took a few minutes to digest the news. Lieutenant Colonel Dimka had been caught in Kano at three o'clock that morning and all the airports were now open again. Eduardo picked up the phone and dialed three digits.

"Manuel, you've heard the news? . . . Good. . . . Then you must fly back with me in my 707 or it may be days before you get out. . . . One hour's time in the lobby . . . See you then."

At eight forty-five there was a quiet knock on the door and Eduardo's secretary opened it to find Colonel Usman standing to attention, just as he had done in the days before the coup. He held a note in his hand. Eduardo tore open the envelope to find an invitation to lunch that day with the new Head of State, General Obasanjo.

"Please convey my apologies to your President," said Eduardo, "and be kind enough to explain that I have pressing commitments to attend to in my own country."

The colonel retired reluctantly. Eduardo dressed in the suit, shirt and tie he had worn on his first day in Nigeria and took the lift downstairs to the lobby, where he joined Manuel, who was once more wearing jeans and a T-shirt. The two chairmen left the hotel and climbed into the back of the leading Mercedes and the motorcade of six began its journey to the airport. The colonel, who now sat in front with the driver, did not venture to speak to either of the distinguished Brazilians for the entire journey. The two men, he would be able to tell the new President later, seemed to be preoccupied with a discussion on an Amazon road project and how the responsibility should be divided between their two companies.

Customs were bypassed as neither man had anything he wanted to take out of the country other than himself, and the fleet of cars came to a halt at the side of Eduardo's blue and silver 707. The staff of both companies climbed aboard the rear section of the aircraft, also engrossed in discussion on the Amazon road project.

A corporal jumped out of the lead car and opened the back door to allow the two chairmen to walk straight up the steps and board the front section of the aircraft.

As Eduardo stepped out of the Mercedes, the Nigerian driver saluted smartly. "Goodbye, sir," he said, revealing the large set of white teeth once again.

Eduardo said nothing.

"I hope," said the corporal politely, "you made very big deal while you were in Nigeria."

Old Love

SOME PEOPLE, it is said, fall in love at first sight, but that was not what happened to William Hatchard and Philippa Jameson. They hated each other from the moment they met. This mutual loathing commenced at the first tutorial of their freshman terms. Both had come up in the early thirties with major scholarships to read English language and literature, William to Merton, Philippa to Somerville. Each had been reliably assured by their schoolteachers that they would be the star pupil of their year.

Their tutor, Simon Jakes of New College, was both bemused and amused by the ferocious competition that so quickly developed between his two brightest pupils, and he used their enmity skillfully to bring out the best in both of them without ever allowing either to indulge in outright abuse. Philippa, an attractive, slim redhead with a rather high-pitched voice, was the same height as William, so she conducted as many of her arguments as possible standing in newly acquired high-heeled shoes, while William, whose deep voice had an air of authority, would always try to expound his opinions from a sitting position. The more intense their rivalry became, the harder the one tried to outdo the other. By the end of their first year they were far ahead of their contemporaries while remaining neck and neck with each other. Simon Jakes told the Merton Professor of Anglo-Saxon Studies that he had never had a brighter pair up in the same year and that it wouldn't be long before they were holding their own with him.

During the long vacation both worked to a grueling timetable, always imagining the other would be doing a little more. They stripped bare Blake, Wordsworth, Coleridge, Shelley, Byron, and only went to bed with Keats. When they returned for the second year, they found that absence had made the heart grow even more hostile; and when they were both awarded alpha plus for their essays on *Beowulf*, it didn't help. Simon Jakes remarked at New College high table one night that if Philippa Jameson had been born a boy some of his tutorials would undoubtedly have ended in blows.

"Why don't you separate them?" asked the Dean, sleepily.

"What, and double my work-load?" said Jakes. "They teach each other most of the time: I merely act as referee."

Occasionally the adversaries would seek his adjudication as to who was ahead of whom, and so confident was each of being the favored pupil that one would always ask in the other's hearing. Jakes was far too canny to be drawn; instead he would remind them that the examiners would be the final arbiters. So they began their own subterfuge by referring to each other, just in earshot, as "that silly woman," and "that arrogant man." By the end of their second year they were almost unable to remain in the same room together.

In the long vacation William took a passing interest in Al Jolson and a girl called Ruby while Philippa flirted with the Charleston and a young naval lieutenant from Dartmouth. But when term started in earnest these interludes were never admitted and soon forgotten.

At the beginning of their third year they both, on Simon Jakes' advice, entered for the Charles Oldham Shakespeare prize along with every other student in the year who was considered likely to gain a First. The Charles Oldham was awarded for an essay on a set aspect of Shakespeare's work, and Philippa and William both realized that this would be the only time in their academic lives that they would be tested against each other in closed competition. Surreptitiously, they worked their separate ways through the entire Shakespearean canon, from *Henry VI* to *Henry VIII*, and kept Jakes well over his appointed tutorial hours, demanding more and more refined discussion of more and more obscure points.

The chosen theme for the prize essay that year was "Satire in Shakespeare." *Troilus and Cressida* clearly called for the most attention, but both found there were nuances in virtually every one of the bard's thirty-seven plays. "Not to mention a gross of sonnets," wrote Philippa home to her father in a rare moment of self-doubt. As the year drew to a close it became obvious to all concerned that either William or Philippa had to win the prize while the other would undoubtedly come in second. Nevertheless no one was willing to venture an opinion as to who the victor would be. The New College porter, an expert in these matters, opening his usual book for the Charles Oldham, made them both evens, ten to one the rest of the field.

Before the prize essay submission date was due, they both had to sit their final degree examinations. Philippa and William confronted the examination papers every morning and afternoon for two weeks with an appetite that bordered on the vulgar. It came as no surprise to anyone that they both achieved first class degrees in the final honors school. Rumor spread around the University that the two rivals had been awarded alphas in every one of their nine papers.

"I am willing to believe that is the case," Philippa told William. "But I feel I must point out to you that there is a considerable difference between an alpha plus and an alpha minus."

"I couldn't agree with you *more*," said William. "And when you discover who has won the Charles Oldham, you will know who was awarded *less*."

With only three weeks left before the prize essay had to be handed in they both worked twelve hours a day, falling asleep over open textbooks, dreaming that the other was still beavering away. When the appointed hour came they met in the marble-floored entrance hall of the Examination Schools, somber in subfusc.

"Good morning, William, I do hope your efforts will manage to secure a place in the first six."

"Thank you, Philippa. If they don't I shall look for the names C. S. Lewis, Nichol Smith, Nevill Coghill, Edmund Blunden, R. W. Chambers and H. W. Garrard ahead of me. There's certainly no one else in the field to worry about."

"I am only pleased," said Philippa, as if she had not heard his reply, "that you were not seated next to me when I wrote my essay, thus ensuring for the first time in three years that you weren't able to crib from my notes."

"The only item I have ever cribbed from you, Philippa, was the Oxford to London timetable, and that I discovered later to be out-of-date, which was in keeping with the rest of your efforts."

They both handed in their 25,000-word essays to the collector's office in the Examination Schools and left without a further word, returning to their respective colleges impatiently to await the result.

William tried to relax the weekend after submitting his essay, and for the first time in three years he played some tennis, against a girl from St. Anne's, failing to win a game, let alone a set. He nearly sank when he went swimming, and actually did so when punting. He was only relieved that Philippa had not been witness to any of his feeble physical efforts.

On Monday night after a resplendent dinner with the Master of Merton, he decided to take a walk along the banks of the Cherwell to clear his head before going to bed. The May evening was still light as he made his way down through the narrow confines of Merton Wall, across the meadows to the banks of the Cherwell. As he strolled along the winding path, he thought he spied his rival ahead of him under a tree reading. He considered turning back but decided she might already have spotted him, so he kept on walking.

He had not seen Philippa for three days although she had rarely been out of his thoughts: once he had won the Charles Oldham, the silly woman would have to climb down from that high horse of hers. He smiled at the thought and decided to walk nonchalantly past her. As he drew nearer, he lifted his eyes from the path in front of him to steal a quick glance in her direction, and could feel himself reddening in anticipation of her inevitable well-timed insult. Nothing happened, so he looked more carefully, only to discover on closer inspection that she was not reading: her head was bowed in her hands and she appeared to be sobbing quietly. He slowed his progress to observe, not the formidable rival who had for three years dogged his every step, but a forlorn and lonely creature who looked somewhat helpless.

William's first reaction was to think that the winner of the prize essay competition had been leaked to her and that he had indeed achieved his victory. On reflection, he realized that could not be the case: the examiners would only have received the essays that morning and since all the assessors read each submission the results could not possibly be forthcoming until at least the end of the week. Philippa did not look up when he reached her side—he was even unsure whether she was aware of his presence. As he stopped to gaze at his adversary William could not help noticing how her long red hair curled just as it touched the shoulder. He sat down beside her but still she did not stir.

"What's the matter?" he asked. "Is there anything I can do?"

She raised her head, revealing a face flushed from crying.

"No, nothing, William, except leave me alone. You deprive me of solitude without affording me company."

William was pleased that he immediately recognized the little literary allusion. "What's the matter, Madame de Sévigné?" he asked, more out of curiosity than concern, torn between sympathy and glee at catching her with her guard down.

It seemed a long time before she replied.

"My father died this morning," she said finally, as if speaking to herself.

It struck William as strange that after three years of seeing Philippa almost every day he knew nothing about her home life.

"And your mother?" he said.

"She died when I was three. I don't even remember her. My father is—" She paused. "Was a parish priest and brought me up, sacrificing everything he had to get me to Oxford, even the family silver. I wanted so much to win the Charles Oldham for him."

William put his arm tentatively on Philippa's shoulder.

"Don't be absurd. When you win the prize, they'll pronounce you the star pupil of the decade. After all, you will have had to beat me to achieve the distinction."

She tried to laugh. "Of course I wanted to beat you, William, but only for my father."

"How did he die?"

"Cancer, only he never let me know. He asked me not to go home before the summer term, as he felt the break might interfere with my finals and the Charles Oldham. While all the time he must have been keeping me away because he knew if I saw the state he was in that would have been the end of my completing any serious work."

"Where do you live?" asked William, again surprised that he did not know.

"Brockenhurst. In Hampshire. I'm going back there tomorrow morning. The funeral's on Wednesday."

"May I take you?" asked William.

Philippa looked up and was aware of a softness in her adversary's eyes that she had not seen before. "That would be kind, William."

"Come on then, you silly woman," he said. "I'll walk you back to your college."

"Last time you called me 'silly woman' you meant it."

William found it natural that they should hold hands as they walked along the river bank. Neither spoke until they reached Somerville.

"What time shall I pick you up?" he asked, not letting go of her hand.

"I didn't know you had a car."

"My father presented me with an old MG when I was awarded a first. I have been longing to find some excuse to show the damn thing off to you. It has a press button start, you know."

"Obviously he didn't want to risk waiting to give you the car on the Charles Oldham results." William laughed more heartily than the little dig merited.

"Sorry," she said. "Put it down to habit. I shall look forward to seeing if you drive as appallingly as you write, in which case the journey may never come to any conclusion. I'll be ready for you at ten."

• • •

On the journey down to Hampshire, Philippa talked about her father's work as a parish priest and inquired after William's family. They stopped for lunch at a pub in Winchester. Rabbit stew and mashed potatoes.

"The first meal we've had together," said William.

No sardonic reply came flying back; Philippa simply smiled.

After lunch they traveled on to the village of Brockenhurst. William brought his car to an uncertain halt on the gravel outside the vicarage. An elderly maid, dressed in black, answered the door, surprised to see Miss Philippa with a man. Philippa introduced Annie to William and asked her to make up the spare room.

"I'm so glad you've found yourself such a nice young man," remarked Annie later. "Have you known him long?"

Philippa smiled. "No, we met for the first time yesterday."

Philippa cooked William dinner, which they ate by a fire he had made up in the front room. Although hardly a word passed between them for three hours, neither was bored. Philippa began to notice the way William's untidy fair hair fell over his forehead and thought how distinguished he would look in old age.

The next morning, she walked into the church on William's arm and stood bravely through the funeral. When the service was over William took her back to the vicarage, crowded with the many friends the parson had made.

"You mustn't think ill of us," said Mr. Crump, the vicar's warden, to Philippa. "You were everything to your father and we were all under strict instructions not to let you know about his illness in case it should interfere with the Charles Oldham. That is the name of the prize, isn't it?"

"Yes," said Philippa. "But that all seems so unimportant now."

"She will win the prize in her father's memory," said William.

Philippa turned and looked at him, realizing for the first time that he actually wanted her to win the Charles Oldham.

They stayed that night at the vicarage and drove back to Oxford on Thursday. On Friday morning at ten o'clock William returned to Philippa's college and asked the porter if he could speak to Miss Jameson.

"Would you be kind enough to wait in the Horsebox, sir," said the porter as he showed William into a little room at the back of the lodge and then scurried off to find Miss Jameson. They returned together a few minutes later.

"What on earth are you doing here?"

"Come to take you to Stratford."

"But I haven't even had time to unpack the things I brought back from Brockenhurst."

"Just do as you are told for once; I'll give you fifteen minutes."

"Of course," she said. "Who am I to disobey the next winner of the Charles Oldham? I shall even allow you to come up to my room for one minute and help me unpack."

The porter's eyebrows nudged the edge of his cap but he remained silent, in deference to Miss Jameson's recent bereavement. Again it surprised William to think that he had never been to Philippa's room during their three years. He had climbed the walls of all the women's colleges to be with a variety of girls of varying stupidity but never with Philippa. He sat down on the end of the bed.

"Not there, you thoughtless creature. The maid has only just made it. Men are all the same, you never sit in chairs."

"I shall one day," said William. "The chair of English Language and Literature."

"Not as long as I'm at this University, you won't," she said, as she disappeared into the bathroom.

"Good intentions are one thing but talent is quite

another," he shouted at her retreating back, privately pleased that her competitive streak seemed to be returning.

Fifteen minutes later she came out of the bathroom in a yellow flowered dress with a neat white collar and matching cuffs. William thought she might even be wearing a touch of make-up.

"It will do our reputations no good to be seen together," she said.

"I've thought about that," said William. "If asked, I shall say you're my charity."

"Your charity?"

"Yes, this year I'm supporting distressed orphans."

Philippa signed out of college until midnight and the two scholars traveled down to Stratford, stopping off at Broadway for lunch. In the afternoon they rowed on the River Avon. William warned Philippa of his last disastrous outing in a punt. She admitted that she had already heard of the exhibition he had made of himself, but they arrived safely back at the shore—perhaps because Philippa took over the rowing. They went to see John Gielgud playing Romeo and dined at the Dirty Duck. Philippa was even quite rude to William during the meal.

They started their journey home just after eleven and Philippa fell into a half sleep as they could hardly hear each other above the noise of the car engine. It must have been about twenty-five miles outside of Oxford that the MG came to a halt.

"I thought," said William, "that when the petrol gauge showed empty there was at least another gallon left in the tank."

"You're obviously wrong, and not for the first time, and because of such foresight you'll have to walk to the nearest garage all by yourself—you needn't imagine that I'm going to keep you company. I intend to stay put, right here in the warmth."

"But there isn't a garage between here and Oxford," protested William.

"Then you'll have to carry me. I am far too fragile to walk."

"I wouldn't be able to manage fifty yards after that sumptuous dinner and all that wine."

"It is no small mystery to me, William, how you could have managed a first class honors degree in English when you can't even read a petrol gauge."

"There's only one thing for it," said William. "We'll have to wait for the first bus in the morning."

Philippa clambered into the back seat and did not speak to him again before falling asleep. William donned his hat, scarf and gloves, crossed his arms for warmth, and touched the tangled red mane of Philippa's hair as she slept. He then took off his coat and placed it so that it covered her.

Philippa woke first, a little after six, and groaned as she tried to stretch her aching limbs. She then shook William awake to ask him why his father hadn't been considerate enough to buy him a car with a comfortable back seat.

"But this is the niftiest thing going," said William, gingerly kneading his neck muscles before putting his coat back on.

"But it isn't going, and won't without petrol," she replied, getting out of the car to stretch her legs.

"But I only let it run out for one reason," said William, following her to the front of the car.

Philippa waited for a feeble punch line and was not disappointed.

"My father told me if I spent the night with a barmaid then I should simply order an extra pint of beer, but if I spent the night with the vicar's daughter, I would have to marry her."

Philippa laughed. William, tired, unshaven, and encumbered by his heavy coat, struggled to get down on one knee.

"What are you doing, William?"

"What do you think I'm doing, you silly woman. I am going to ask you to marry me."

"An invitation I am happy to decline, William. If I accepted such a proposal I might end up spending the rest of my life stranded on the road between Oxford and Stratford."

"Will you marry me if I win the Charles Oldham?"

"As there is absolutely no fear of that happening I can safely say, yes. Now do get off your knee, William, before someone mistakes you for a straying stork."

The first bus arrived at five past seven that Saturday morning and took Philippa and William back to Oxford. Philippa went to her rooms for a long hot bath while William filled a petrol can and returned to his deserted MG. Having completed the task, he drove straight to Somerville and once again asked if he could see Miss Jameson. She came down a few minutes later.

"What, you again?" she said. "Am I not in enough trouble already?"

"Why so?"

"Because I was out after midnight, unaccompanied."

"You were accompanied."

"Yes, and that's what's worrying them."

"Did you tell them we spent the night together?"

"No, I did not. I don't mind our contemporaries thinking I'm promiscuous, but I have strong objections to their believing that I have no taste. Now kindly go away, as I am contemplating the horror of your winning the Charles Oldham and my having to spend the rest of my life with you."

"You know I'm bound to win, so why don't you come live with me now?"

"I realize that it has become fashionable to sleep with just anyone nowadays, William, but if this is to be my last weekend of freedom I intend to savor it, especially as I may have to consider committing suicide."

"I love you."

"For the last time, William, go away. And if you haven't won the Charles Oldham don't ever show your face in Somerville again."

William left, desperate to know the result of the prize essay competition. Had he realized how much Philippa wanted him to win, he might have slept that night.

On Monday morning they both arrived early in the Examination Schools and stood waiting impatiently without speaking to each other, jostled by the other undergraduates of their year who had also been entered for the prize. On the stroke of ten the chairman of the examiners, in full academic dress, walking at tortoise-like pace, arrived in the great hall and with a considerable pretense at indifference pinned a notice to the board. All the undergraduates who had entered for the prize rushed forward except for William and Philippa who stood alone, aware that it was now too late to influence a result they were both dreading.

A girl shot out from the melee around the notice board and ran over to Philippa.

"Well done, Phil. You've won."

Tears came to Philippa's eyes as she turned toward William.

"May I add my congratulations," he said quickly. "You obviously deserved the prize."

"I wanted to say something to you on Saturday."

"You did, you said if I lost I must never show my face in Somerville again."

"No, I wanted to say: I do love nothing in the world so well as you; is not that strange?"

He looked at her silently for a long moment. It was

impossible to improve upon Beatrice's reply.

"As strange as the thing I know not," he said softly.

A college friend slapped him on the shoulder, took his hand and shook it vigorously. *Proxime accessit* was obviously impressive in some people's eyes, if not in William's.

"Well done, William."

"Second place is not worthy of praise," said William disdainfully.

"But you won, Billy boy."

Philippa and William stared at each other.

"What do you mean?" said William.

"Exactly what I said. You've won the Charles Oldham."

Philippa and William ran to the board and studied the notice.

Charles Oldham Memorial Prize
The examiners felt unable on this occasion to award the prize to one person and have therefore decided that it should be shared by

They gazed at the notice board in silence for some moments. Finally, Philippa bit her lip and said in a small voice:

"Well, you didn't do too badly, considering the competition. I'm prepared to honor my undertaking but by this light I take thee for pity."

William needed no prompting. "I would not deny you, but by this good day I yield upon great persuasion, for I was told you were in a consumption."

And to the delight of their peers and the amazement of the retreating don, they embraced under the notice board.

Rumor had it that from that moment on they were never apart for more than a few hours.

• • •

The marriage took place a month later in Philippa's family church at Brockenhurst. "Well, when you think about it," said William's roommate, "who else could she have married?" The contentious couple started their honeymoon in Athens arguing about the relative significance of Doric and Ionic architecture, of which neither knew any more than they had covertly conned from a half-crown tourist guide. They sailed on to Istanbul, where William prostrated himself at the front of every mosque he could find while Philippa stood on her own at the back fuming at the Turks' treatment of women.

"The Turks are a shrewd race," declared William, "so quick to understand real values."

"Then why don't you embrace the Moslem religion, William, and I need be in your presence only once a year."

"The misfortune of birth, a misplaced loyalty and the signing of an unfortunate contract dictate that I spend the rest of my life with you."

Back at Oxford, with junior research fellowships at their respective colleges, they settled down to serious creative work. William embarked upon a massive study of word usage in Marlowe and, in his spare moments, taught himself statistics to assist his findings. Philippa chose as her subject the influence of the Reformation on seventeenth-century English writers and was soon drawn beyond literature into art and music. She bought herself a spinet and took to playing Dowland and Gibbons in the evening.

"For Christ's sake," said William, exasperated by the tinny sound, "you won't deduce their religious convictions from their key signatures."

"More informative than ifs and ands, my dear," she said, imperturbably, "and at night so much more relaxing than pots and pans."

Three years later, with well-received D. Phils, they

moved on, inexorably in tandem, to college teaching fellowships. As the long shadow of fascism fell across Europe, they read, wrote, criticized and coached by quiet firesides in unchanging quadrangles.

"A rather dull Schools year for me," said William, "but I still managed five firsts from a field of eleven."

"An even duller one for me," said Philippa, "but somehow I squeezed three firsts out of six, and you won't have to invoke the binomial theorem, William, to work out that it's an arithmetical victory for me."

"The chairman of the examiners tells me," said William, "that a greater part of what your pupils say is no more than a recitation from memory."

"He told me," she retorted, "that yours have to make it up as they go along."

When they dined together in college the guest list was always quickly filled, and as soon as grace had been said, the sharpness of their dialogue would flash across the candelabra.

"I hear a rumor, Philippa, that the college doesn't feel able to renew your fellowship at the end of the year?"

"I fear you speak the truth, William," she replied. "They decided they couldn't renew mine at the same time as offering me yours."

"Do you think they will ever make you a Fellow of the British Academy, William?"

"I must say, with some considerable disappointment, never."

"I am sorry to hear that; why not?"

"Because when they did invite me, I informed the President that I would prefer to wait to be elected at the same time as my wife."

Some non-University guests sitting in high table for the first time took their verbal battles seriously; others could only be envious of such love.

One Fellow uncharitably suggested they rehearsed their lines before coming to dinner for fear it might be thought they were getting on well together. During their early years as young dons, they became acknowledged as the leaders in their respective fields. Like magnets, they attracted the brightest undergraduates while apparently remaining poles apart themselves.

"Dr. Hatchard will be delivering half these lectures," Philippa announced at the start of the Michaelmas Term of their joint lecture course on Arthurian legend. "But I can assure you it will not be the better half. You would be wise always to check which Dr. Hatchard is lecturing."

When Philippa was invited to give a series of lectures at Yale, William took a sabbatical so that he could be with her.

On the ship crossing the Atlantic, Philippa said, "Let's at least be thankful the journey is by sea, my dear, so we can't run out of petrol."

"Rather let us thank God," replied William, "that the ship has an engine because you would even take the wind out of Cunard's sails."

The only sadness in their lives was that Philippa could bear William no children, but if anything it drew the two closer together. Philippa lavished quasi-maternal affection on her tutorial pupils and allowed herself only the wry comment that she was spared the probability of producing a child with William's looks and William's brains.

At the outbreak of war William's expertise with handling words made a move into cipher-breaking inevitable. He was recruited by an anonymous gentleman who visited them at home with a briefcase chained to his wrist. Philippa listened shamelessly at the keyhole while they discussed the problems they had come up against and burst into the room and demanded to be recruited as well.

"Do you realize that I can complete *The Times* crossword puzzle in half the time my husband can?"

The anonymous man was only thankful that he wasn't chained to Philippa. He drafted them both to the Admiralty section to deal with enciphered wireless messages to and from German submarines.

The German signal manual was a four-letter code book and each message was reciphered, the substitution table changing daily. William taught Philippa how to evaluate letter frequencies and she applied her new knowledge to modern German texts, coming up with a frequency analysis that was soon used by every code-breaking department in the Commonwealth.

Even so, breaking the ciphers and building up the master signal book was a colossal task which took them the best part of two years.

"I never knew your ifs and ands could be so informative," she said admiringly of her own work.

When the allies invaded Europe, husband and wife could together often break ciphers with no more than half a dozen lines of encoded text to go on.

"They're an illiterate lot," grumbled William. "They don't encipher their umlauts. They deserve to be misunderstood."

"How can you give an opinion when you never dot your i's, William?"

"Because I consider the dot is redundant and I hope to be responsible for removing it from the English language."

"Is that to be your major contribution to scholarship, William? If so, I am bound to ask how anyone reading the work of most of our undergraduates' essays would be able to tell the difference between an l and an i."

"A feeble argument, my dear, that if it had any conviction would demand that you put a dot on top of an n so as to be sure it wasn't mistaken for an h."

"Keep working away at your theories, William, because

I intend to spend my energy removing more than the dot and the l from Hitler."

In May 1945 they dined privately with the Prime Minister and Mrs. Churchill at Number Ten Downing Street.

"What did the Prime Minister mean when he said to me he could never understand what you were up to?" asked Philippa in the taxi to Paddington Station.

"The same as when he said to me he knew exactly what you were capable of, I suppose," said William.

When the Merton Professor of English retired in the early nineteen-fifties the whole University waited to see which Dr. Hatchard would be appointed to the chair.

"If Council invite you to take the chair," said William, putting his hand through his graying hair, "it will be because they are going to make me Vice-Chancellor."

"The only way you could ever be invited to hold a position so far beyond your ability would be nepotism, which would mean I was already Vice-Chancellor."

The General Board, after several hours' discussion of the problem, offered two chairs and appointed William and Philippa full professors on the same day.

When the Vice-Chancellor was asked why precedent had been broken he replied: "Simple; if I hadn't given them both a chair, one of them would have been after my job."

That night, after a celebration dinner when they were walking home together along the banks of the Isis across Christ Church Meadows, in the midst of a particularly heated argument about the quality of the last volume of Proust's monumental works, a policeman, noticing the affray, ran over to them and asked:

"Is everything all right, madam?"

"No, it is not," William interjected. "This woman has been attacking me for thirty years and to date the police have done deplorably little to protect me."

In the late fifties Harold Macmillan invited Philippa to join the board of the IBA.

"I suppose you'll become what's known as a telly don," said William, "and as the average mental age of those who watch the box is seven you should feel quite at home."

"Agreed," said Philippa. "Over twenty years of living with you has made me fully qualified to deal with infants."

The chairman of the BBC wrote to William a few weeks later inviting him to join the Board of Governors.

"Are you to replace 'Hancock's Half Hour' or 'Dick Barton, Special Agent'?" Philippa inquired.

"I am to give a series of twelve lectures."

"On what subject, pray?"

"Genius."

Philippa flicked through the *Radio Times*. "I see that 'Genius' is to be viewed at two o'clock on a Sunday morning, which is understandable, as it's when you are at your most brilliant."

When William was awarded an honorary doctorate at Princeton, Philippa attended the ceremony and sat proudly in the front row.

"I tried to secure a place at the back," she explained, "but it was filled with sleeping students who had obviously never heard of you."

"If that's the case, Philippa, I am only surprised you didn't mistake them for one of your tutorial lectures."

As the years passed, many anecdotes, only some of which were apocryphal, passed into the Oxford fabric. Everyone in the English school knew the stories about the "fighting Hatchards." How they spent their first night together. How they jointly won the Charles Oldham. How Phil would complete *The Times* crossword before Bill had finished shaving. How they were both appointed to professorial chairs on the same day, and worked longer hours than any of their contemporaries as if they still had something to prove, if only to each other. It seemed almost required by the laws of symmetry that they should always be judged equals. Until it was announced in the New Year's Honors that Philippa had been made a Dame of the British Empire.

"At least our dear Queen has worked out which one of us is truly worthy of recognition," she said over the college dessert.

"Our dear Queen," said William, selecting the Madeira, "knows only too well how little competition there is in the women's colleges: sometimes one must encourage weaker candidates in the hope that it might inspire some real talent lower down."

After that, whenever they attended a public function together, Philippa would have the M.C. announce them as Professor William and Dame Philippa Hatchard. She looked forward to many happy years of starting every official occasion one up on her husband, but her triumph lasted for only six months as William received a knighthood in the Queen's Birthday Honors. Philippa feigned surprise at the dear Queen's uncharacteristic lapse of judgment and forthwith insisted on their being introduced in public as Sir William and Dame Philippa Hatchard.

"Understandable," said William. "The Queen had to make you a Dame first in order that no one should mistake you for a lady. When I married you, Philippa, you were a young fellow, and now I find I'm living with an old Dame."

"It's no wonder," said Philippa, "that your poor pupils can't make up their minds whether you're homosexual or you simply have a mother fixation. Be thankful that I did not accept Girton's invitation: then you would have been married to a mistress."

"I always have been, you silly woman."

As the years passed, they never let up their pretended

belief in each other's mental feebleness. Philippa's books, "works of considerable distinction," she insisted, were published by Oxford University Press while William's "works of monumental significance," he declared, were printed at the presses of Cambridge University.

The tally of newly appointed professors of English they had taught as undergraduates soon reached double figures.

"If you will count polytechnics, I shall have to throw in Maguire's readership in Kenya," said William.

"You did not teach the Professor of English at Nairobi," said Philippa. "I did. You taught the Head of State, which may well account for why the University is so highly thought of while the country is in such disarray."

In the early sixties they conducted a battle of letters in the *Times Literary Supplement* on the works of Philip Sidney without ever discussing the subject in each other's presence. In the end the editor said the correspondence must stop and adjudicated a draw.

They both declared him an idiot.

If there was one act that annoyed William in old age about Philippa, it was her continued determination each morning to complete *The Times* crossword before he arrived at the breakfast table. For a time, William ordered two copies of the paper, until Philippa filled them both in while explaining to him it was a waste of money.

One particular morning in June at the end of their final academic year before retirement, William came down to breakfast to find only one space in the crossword left for him to complete. He studied the clue: "Skelton reported that this landed in the soup." He immediately filled in the eight little boxes.

Philippa looked over his shoulder. "There's no such word, you arrogant man," she said firmly. "You made it up to annoy me." She placed in front of him a very hard boiled egg.

"Of course there is, you silly woman; look whym-wham up in the dictionary."

Philippa checked in the *Oxford Shorter* among the cookery books in the kitchen, and trumpeted her delight that it was nowhere to be found.

"My dear Dame Philippa," said William, as if he were addressing a particularly stupid pupil, "you surely cannot imagine because you are old and your hair has become very white that you are a sage. You must understand that the Shorter Oxford Dictionary was cobbled together for simpletons whose command of the English language stretches to no more than one hundred thousand words. When I go to college this morning I shall confirm the existence of the word in the O.E.D. on my desk. Need I remind you that the O.E.D. is a serious work which, with over five hundred thousand words, was designed for scholars like myself?"

"Rubbish," said Philippa. "When I am proved right, you will repeat this story word for word, including your offensive non-word, at Somerville's Gaudy Feast."

"And you, my dear, will read the Collected Works of John Skelton and eat humble pie as your first course."

"We'll ask old Onions along to adjudicate."

"Agreed."

"Agreed."

With that, Sir William picked up his paper, kissed his wife on the cheek and said with an exaggerated sigh, "It's at times like this that I wish I'd lost the Charles Oldham."

"You did, my dear. It was in the days when it wasn't fashionable to admit a woman had won anything."

"You won me."

"Yes, you arrogant man, but I was led to believe you were one of those prizes one could return at the end of the year. And now I find I shall have to keep you, even in retirement."

"Let us leave it to the Oxford English Dictionary, my

dear, to decide the issue the Charles Oldham examiners were unable to determine." And with that he departed for his college.

"There's no such word," Philippa muttered as he closed the front door.

Heart attacks are known to be rarer among women than among men. When Dame Philippa suffered hers in the kitchen that morning she collapsed on the floor calling hoarsely for William, but he was already out of earshot. It was the cleaning woman who found Dame Philippa on the kitchen floor and ran to fetch someone in authority. The Bursar's first reaction was that she was probably pretending that Sir William had hit her with a frying pan, but nevertheless she hurried over to the Hatchards' house in Little Jericho just in case. The Bursar checked Dame Philippa's pulse and called for the college doctor and then the Principal. Both arrived within minutes.

The Principal and the Bursar stood waiting by the side of their illustrious academic colleague, but they already knew what the doctor was going to say.

"She's dead," he confirmed. "It must have been very sudden and with the minimum of pain." He checked his watch; the time was nine forty-seven. He covered his patient with a blanket and called for an ambulance. He had taken care of Dame Philippa for more than thirty years and he had told her so often to slow down that he might as well have made a gramophone record of it for all the notice she took.

"Who will tell Sir William?" asked the Principal. The three of them looked at each other.

"I will," said the doctor.

It's a short walk from Little Jericho to Radcliffe Square. It was a long walk from Little Jericho to Radcliffe Square for the doctor that day. He never relished telling anyone of the death of a spouse, but this one was going to be the unhappiest of his career.

When he knocked on the professor's door, Sir William bade him enter. The great man was sitting at his desk poring over the Oxford Dictionary, humming to himself.

"I told her, but she wouldn't listen, the silly woman," he was saying to himself, and then he turned and saw the doctor standing silently in the doorway. "Doctor, you must be my guest at Somerville's Gaudy next Thursday week where Dame Philippa will be eating humble pie. It will be nothing less than game, set, match and championship for me. A vindication of thirty years' scholarship."

The doctor did not smile, nor did he stir. Sir William walked over to him and gazed at his old friend intently. No words were necessary. The doctor said only, "I'm more sorry than I am able to express," and he left Sir William to his private grief.

Sir William's colleagues all knew within the hour. College lunch that day was spent in a silence broken only by the Senior Tutor inquiring of the Master if some food should be taken up to the Merton professor.

"I think not," said the Master. Nothing more was said.

Professors, Fellows and students alike crossed the front quadrangle in silence and when they gathered for dinner that evening still no one felt like conversation. At the end of the meal the Senior Tutor suggested once again that something should be taken up to Sir William. This time the Master nodded his agreement and a light meal was prepared by the college chef. The Master and the Senior Tutor climbed the worn stone steps to Sir William's room and while one held the tray the other gently knocked on the door. There was no reply, so the Master, used to William's ways, pushed the door ajar and looked in.

The old man lay motionless on the wooden floor in a pool of blood, a small pistol by his side. The two men walked in and stared down. In his right hand, William was holding the Collected Works of John Skelton. The book was opened at *The Tunnyng of Elynour Rummyng*, and the word "whym-wham" was underlined.

a 1529, Skelton, *E. Rummyng* 75

After the Sarasyns gyse,
Woth a whym wham,
Knyt with a trym tram,
Upon her brayne pan.

Sir William, in his neat hand, had written a note in the margin: "Forgive me, but I had to let her know."

"Know what, I wonder?" said the Master softly to himself as he attempted to remove the book from Sir William's hand, but the fingers were already stiff and cold around it.

Legend has it that they were never apart for more than a few hours.

The Perfect Gentleman

I WOULD NEVER HAVE MET Edward Shrimpton if he hadn't needed a towel. He stood naked by my side staring down at the bench in front of him, muttering, "I could have sworn I left the damn thing there."

I had just come out of the sauna, swathed in towels, so I took one off my shoulder and passed it to him. He thanked me and put out his hand.

"Edward Shrimpton," he said, smiling. I took his hand and wondered what we must have looked like standing there in the gymnasium locker room of the Metropolitan Club in the early evening, two grown men shaking hands in the nude.

"I don't remember seeing you in the club before," he added.

"No, I'm an overseas member."

"Ah, from England. What brings you to New York?"

"I'm pursuing an American novelist whom my company would like to publish in England."

"And are you having any success?"

"Yes, I think I'll close the deal this week—as long as the agent stops trying to convince me that his author is a cross between Tolstoy and Dickens and should be paid accordingly."

"Neither was paid particularly well, if I remember correctly," offered Edward Shrimpton as he energetically rubbed the towel up and down his back.

"A fact I pointed out to the agent at the time, who only countered by reminding me that it was my house who had published Dickens originally."

"I suggest," said Edward Shrimpton, "that you *remind* him that the end result turned out to be successful for all concerned."

"I did, but I fear this agent is more interested in 'up front' than posterity."

"As a banker that's a sentiment of which I could hardly disapprove, since the one thing we have in common with publishers is that our clients are always trying to tell us a good tale."

"Perhaps you should sit down and write one of them for me?" I said politely.

"Heaven forbid, you must be sick of being told that there's a book in every one of us, so I hasten to assure you that there isn't one in me."

I laughed, as I found it refreshing not to be informed by a new acquaintance that his memoirs, if only he could find the time to write them, would overnight be one of the world's best sellers.

"Perhaps there's a story in you, but you're just not aware of it," I suggested.

"If that's the case, I'm afraid it's passed me by."

Mr. Shrimpton re-emerged from behind the row of little tin cubicles and handed me back my towel. He was now fully dressed and stood, I would have guessed, a shade under six feet. He wore a Wall Street banker's pinstripe suit and, although he was nearly bald, he had a remarkable physique for a man who must have been well into his sixties. Only his thick white mustache gave away his true age, and would have been more in keeping with a retired English colonel than a New York banker.

"Are you going to be in New York long?" he inquired, as he took a small leather case from his inside pocket and removed a pair of half-moon spectacles and placed them on the end of his nose.

"Just for the week."

"I don't suppose you're free for lunch tomorrow, by any chance?" he inquired, peering over the top of his glasses.

"Yes, I am. I certainly can't face another meal with that agent."

"Good, then why don't you join me so that I can follow the continuing drama of capturing the elusive American Author?"

"And perhaps I'll discover there is a story in you after all."

"Not a hope," he said. "You would be backing a loser if you depend on that." And once again he offered his hand. "One o'clock, members' dining room suit you?"

"One o'clock, members' dining room," I repeated.

As he left the locker room I walked over to the mirror and straightened my tie. I was dining that night with Eric McKenzie, a publishing friend, who had originally proposed me for membership in the club. To be accurate, Eric McKenzie was my father's friend rather than my own. They had met just before the war while on holiday in Portugal and when I was elected to the club, soon after my father's retirement, Eric took it upon himself to have dinner with me whenever I was in New York. One's parents' generation never see one as anything but a child who will always be in need of constant care and attention. As he was a contemporary of my father, Eric must have been nearly seventy and, although hard of hearing and slightly bent, he was always amusing and good company, even if he did continually ask me if I was aware that his grandfather was Scottish.

As I strapped on my watch, I checked that he was due to arrive in a few minutes. I put on my jacket and strolled out into the hall to find that he was already there, waiting for me. Eric was killing time by reading the out-of-date club notices. Americans, I have observed, can always be relied upon to arrive early or late; never on time. I stood staring at the stooped man, whose hair but for a few strands had now turned silver. His three-piece suit had a button missing on the jacket, which reminded me that his wife had died last year. After another thrust-out hand and exchange of welcomes, we took the lift to the second floor and walked to the dining room.

The members' dining room at the Metropolitan differs little from any other men's club. It has a fair sprinkling of old leather chairs, old carpets, old portraits and old members. A waiter guided us to a corner table which overlooked Central Park. We ordered, and then settled back to discuss all the subjects I found I usually cover with an acquaintance I only have the chance to catch up with a couple of times a year—our families, children, mutual friends, work; baseball and cricket. By the time we had reached cricket we had also reached coffee, so we strolled down to the far end of the room and made ourselves comfortable in two well-worn leather chairs. When the coffee arrived I ordered two brandies and watched Eric unwrap a large Cuban cigar. Although they displayed a West Indian band on the outside, I knew they were Cuban because I had picked them up for him from a tobacconist in St. James's, Piccadilly, which specializes in changing the labels for its American customers. I have often thought that it must be the only shop in the world that changes labels with the sole purpose of making a superior product appear inferior. I am certain my wine merchant does it the other way round.

While Eric was attempting to light the cigar, my eyes wandered to a board on the wall. To be more accurate, it was a highly polished wooden plaque with oblique golden lettering painted on it, honoring those men who over the years had won the club's Backgammon Championship. I glanced idly down the list, not expecting to see anybody with whom I would be familiar, when I was brought up by the name of Edward Shrimpton. Once in the late thirties he had been the runner-up.

"That's interesting," I said.

"What is?" asked Eric, now wreathed in enough smoke to have puffed himself out of Grand Central Station.

"Edward Shrimpton was runner-up in the club's Backgammon Championship in the late thirties. I'm having lunch with him tomorrow."

"I didn't realize you knew him."

"I didn't until this afternoon," I said, and then explained how we had met.

Eric laughed and turned to stare up at the board. Then he added, rather mysteriously: "That's a night I'm never likely to forget."

"Why?" I asked.

Eric hesitated, and looked uncertain of himself before continuing: "Too much water has passed under the bridge for anyone to care now." He paused again, as a hot piece of ash fell to the floor and added to the burn marks that made their own mosaic pattern in the carpet. "Just before the war Edward Shrimpton was among the best half dozen backgammon players in the world. In fact, it must have been around that time he won the unofficial world championship in Monte Carlo."

"And he couldn't win the club championship?"

" 'Couldn't' would be the wrong word, dear boy.

'Didn't' might be more accurate." Eric lapsed into another preoccupied silence.

"Are you going to explain?" I asked, hoping he would continue, "or am I to be left like a child who wants to know who killed Cock Robin?"

"All in good time, but first allow me to get this damn cigar started."

I remained silent and four matches later, he said, "Before I begin, take a look at the man sitting over there in the corner with the young blonde."

I turned and glanced back toward the dining room area, and saw a man attacking a porterhouse steak. He looked about the same age as Eric and wore a smart new suit that was unable to disguise that he had a weight problem: only his tailor could have smiled at him with any pleasure. He was seated opposite a slight, not unattractive strawberry blonde of half his age who could have trodden on a beetle and failed to crush it.

"What an unlikely pair. Who are they?"

"Harry Newman and his fourth wife. They're always the same. The wives, I mean—blond hair, blue eyes, ninety pounds and dumb. I can never understand why any man gets divorced only to marry a carbon copy of the original."

"Where does Edward Shrimpton fit into the jigsaw?" I asked, trying to guide Eric back onto the subject.

"Patience, patience," said my host, as he relit his cigar for the second time. "At your age you've far more time to waste than I have."

I laughed and picked up the cognac nearest to me and swirled the brandy around in my cupped hands.

"Harry Newman," continued Eric, now almost hidden in smoke, "was the fellow who beat Edward Shrimpton in the final of the club championship that year, although in truth he was never in the same class as Edward."

"Do explain," I said, as I looked up at the board to

check that it was Newman's name that preceded Edward Shrimpton's.

"Well," said Eric, "after the semi-final, which Edward had won with consummate ease, we all assumed the final would only be a formality. Harry had always been a good player, but as I had been the one to lose to him in the semi-finals, I knew he couldn't hope to survive a contest with Edward Shrimpton. The club final is won by the first man to twenty-one points, and if I had been asked for an opinion at the time I would have reckoned the result would end up around 21–5 in Edward's favor. Damn cigar," he said, and lit it for a fourth time. Once again I waited impatiently.

"The final is always held on a Saturday night, and poor Harry over there," said Eric, pointing his cigar toward the far corner of the room while depositing some more ash on the floor, "who all of us thought was doing rather well in the insurance business, had a bankruptcy notice served on him the Monday morning before the final—I might add through no fault of his own. His partner had cashed in his stock without Harry's knowledge, disappeared, and left him with all the bills to pick up. Everyone in the club was sympathetic.

"On Thursday the press got hold of the story, and for good measure they added that Harry's wife had run off with the partner. Harry didn't show his head in the club all week, and some of us wondered if he would scratch from the final and let Edward win by default since the result was such a foregone conclusion anyway. But the Games Committee received no communication from Harry to suggest the contest was off, so they proceeded as though nothing had happened. On the night of the final, I dined with Edward Shrimpton here in the club. He was in fine form. He ate very little and drank nothing but a glass of water. If you had asked me then, I wouldn't have put a penny on Harry Newman even if the odds had been ten to one.

"We all dined upstairs on the third floor, since the Committee had cleared this room so that they could seat sixty in a square around the board. The final was due to start at nine o'clock. By twenty to nine there wasn't a seat left in the place, and members were already standing two deep behind the square: it wasn't every day we had the chance to see a world champion in action. By five to nine, Harry still hadn't turned up and some of the members were beginning to get a little restless. As nine o'clock chimed, the referee went over to Edward and had a word with him. I saw Edward shake his head in disagreement and walk away. Just at the point when I thought the referee would have to be firm and award the match to Edward, Harry strolled in looking very dapper, adorned in a dinner jacket several sizes smaller than the suit he is wearing tonight. Edward went straight up to him, shook him warmly by the hand, and together they walked into the center of the room. Even with the throw of the first dice there was a tension about that match. Members were waiting to see how Harry would fare in the opening game."

The intermittent cigar went out again. I leaned over and struck a match for him.

"Thank you, dear boy. Now, where was I? Oh, yes, the first game. Well, Edward only just won the first game and I wondered if he wasn't concentrating or if perhaps he had become a little too relaxed while waiting for his opponent. In the second game the dice ran well for Harry and he won fairly easily. From that moment on it became a finely fought battle, and by the time the score had reached 11–9 in Edward's favor the tension in the room was quite electric. By the ninth game I began watching more carefully and noticed that Edward allowed himself to be drawn into a back game, a small error in judgment that only a seasoned player would have spotted. I wondered how many more subtle errors had already passed that I hadn't observed. Harry went on to win the ninth, making the score 18–17 in his favor. I watched even more diligently as Edward did just enough to win the tenth game and, with a rash double, just enough to lose the eleventh, bring the score to 20 all, so that everything would depend on the final game. I swear that nobody had left the room that evening, and not one back remained against a chair; some members were even hanging on to the window ledges. The room was now full of drink and thick with cigar smoke, and yet when Harry picked up the dice cup for the last game you could hear the little squares of ivory rattle before they hit the board. The dice ran well for Harry in that final game and Edward only made one small error early on that I was able to pick up; but it was enough to give Harry game, match and championship. After the last throw of the dice everyone in that room, including Edward, gave the new champion a standing ovation."

"Had many other members worked out what had really happened that night?"

"No, I don't think so," said Eric. "And certainly Harry Newman hadn't. The talk afterward was that Harry had never played a better game in his life and what a worthy champion he was, all the more for the difficulties he labored under."

"Did Edward have anything to say?"

"Toughest match he'd been in since Monte Carlo and only hoped he would be given the chance to avenge the defeat next year."

"But he wasn't," I said, looking up again at the board. "He never won the club championship."

"That's right. After Roosevelt had insisted we help you guys out in England, the club didn't hold the competition again until 1946, and by then Edward had been to war and had lost all interest in the game."

"And Harry?"

"Oh, Harry. Harry never looked back after that; must have made a dozen deals in the club that night. Within a year he was on top again and even found himself another cute little blonde."

"What does Edward say about the result now, thirty years later?"

"Do you know, that remains a mystery to this day. I have never heard him mention the game once in all that time."

Eric's cigar had come to the end of its working life and he stubbed the remains out in an ashless ashtray. It obviously acted as a signal to remind him that it was time to go home. He rose a little unsteadily and I walked down with him to the front door.

"Goodbye, my boy," he said, "do give Edward my best wishes when you have lunch with him tomorrow. And remember not to play him at backgammon. He'd still kill you."

The next day I arrived in the front hall a few minutes before our appointed time, not sure if Edward Shrimpton would fall into the category of early or late Americans. As the clock struck one, he walked through the door: there has to be an exception to every rule. We agreed to go straight up to lunch since he had to be back on Wall Street for a two-thirty appointment. We stepped into the packed lift. The doors closed like a tired concertina and the slowest lift in America made its way toward the second floor.

As we entered the dining room, I was amused to see that Harry Newman was already there, attacking another steak, while the little blonde lady was nibbling a salad. He waved expansively at Edward Shrimpton, who returned the gesture with a friendly nod. We sat down at a table in the center of the room and studied the menu. Steak and kidney pie was the dish of the day, which was probably the case in half the men's clubs in the world. Edward wrote down our orders in a neat and legible hand on the little white slip provided by the waiter.

Edward asked me about the author I was chasing and made some penetrating comments about her earlier work, to which I responded as best I could while trying to think of a plot to make him discuss the pre-war backgammon championship, which I thought would make a far better story than anything she had ever written. But he never talked about himself once during the meal, so I despaired. Finally, staring up at the plaque on the wall, I said clumsily:

"I see you were runner-up in the club backgammon championship just before the war. You must have been a fine player."

"No, not really," he replied. "Not many people bothered about the game in those days. There is a different attitude today with all the youngsters taking it so seriously."

"What about the champion?" I said, pushing my luck.

"Harry Newman? He was an outstanding player, and particularly good under pressure. He's the gentleman who greeted us when we came in. That's him sitting over there in the corner with his wife."

I looked obediently toward Mr. Newman's table but my host added nothing more, so I gave up. We ordered coffee and that would have been the end of Edward's story if Harry Newman and his wife had not headed straight for us after they had finished their lunch. Edward was on his feet long before I was, despite my twenty-year advantage. Harry Newman looked even bigger standing up, and his little blonde wife looked more like the dessert than his spouse.

"Ed," he boomed, "how are you?"

"I'm well, thank you, Harry," Edward replied. "May I introduce my guest?"

"Nice to know you," he said. "Rusty, I've always

wanted you to meet Ed Shrimpton because I've talked to you about him so often in the past."

"Have you, Harry?" she squeaked.

"Of course. You remember, honey. Ed is up there on the backgammon honors board," he said, pointing a stubby finger toward the plaque. "With only one name in front of him and that's mine. And Ed was the world champion at the time. Isn't that right, Ed?"

"That's right, Harry."

"So I suppose I really should have been the world champion that year, wouldn't you say?"

"I couldn't quarrel with that conclusion," replied Edward.

"On the big day, Rusty, when it really mattered, and the pressure was on, I beat him fair and square."

I stood in silent disbelief as Edward Shrimpton still volunteered no disagreement.

"We must play again for old times' sake, Ed," the fat man continued. "It would be fun to see if you could beat me now. Mind you, I'm a bit rusty nowadays, Rusty." He laughed loudly at his own joke but his spouse's face remained blank. I wondered how long it would be before there was a fifth Mrs. Newman.

"It's been great to see you again, Ed. Take care of yourself."

"Thank you, Harry," said Edward.

We both sat down again as Newman and his wife left the dining room. Our coffee was now cold, so we ordered a fresh pot. The room was almost empty and when I had poured two cups for us Edward leaned over to me conspiratorially and whispered:

"Now there's a hell of a story for a publisher like you. I mean the real truth about Harry Newman."

My ears pricked up as I anticipated his version of the story of what had actually happened on the night of that pre-war backgammon championship more than thirty years before.

"Really?" I said, innocently.

"Oh, yes," said Edward. "It was not as simple as you might think. Just before the war Harry was let down very badly by his business partner, who not only stole his money, but for good measure his wife as well. The very week that he was at his lowest he won the club backgammon championship, put all his troubles behind him and, against the odds, made a brilliant comeback. You know, he's worth a fortune today. Now, wouldn't you agree that that would make one hell of a story?"

Broken Routine

SEPTIMUS HORATIO CORNWALLIS did not live up to his name. With such a name he should have been a cabinet minister, an admiral, or at least a rural dean. In fact, Septimus Horatio Cornwallis was a claims adjuster at the head office of the Prudential Assurance Company Limited, 172 Holborn Bars, London EC1.

Septimus's names could be blamed on his father, who had a small knowledge of Nelson, on his mother, who was superstitious, and on his great-great-great-grandfather, who was alleged to have been a second cousin of the illustrious Governor-General of India. On leaving school, Septimus, a thin, anemic young man prematurely balding, joined the Prudential Assurance Company, his careers master having told him that it was an ideal opening for a young man with his qualifications. Some time later, when Septimus reflected on the advice, it worried him, because even he realized that he had no qualifications. Despite this setback, Septimus rose slowly over the years from office boy to claims adjuster (not so much climbing the ladder as resting upon each rung for some considerable time), which afforded him the grandiose title of assistant deputy manager (claims department).

Septimus spent his day in a glass cubicle on the sixth floor, adjusting claims and recommending payments of anything up to one million pounds. He felt if he kept his nose clean (one of Septimus's favorite expressions), he would, after another twenty years, become a manager (claims department) and have walls around him that you couldn't see through and a carpet that wasn't laid in small squares of slightly differing shades of green. He might even become one of those signatures on the million-pound checks.

Septimus resided in Sevenoaks with his wife, Norma, and his two children, Winston and Elizabeth, who attended the local comprehensive school. They would have gone to the grammar school, he regularly informed his colleagues, but the Labor government had stopped all that.

Septimus operated his daily life by means of a set of invariant sub-routines, like a primitive microprocessor, while he supposed himself to be a great follower of tradition and discipline. For if he was nothing, he was at least a creature of habit. Had, for some inexplicable reason, the K.G.B. wanted to assassinate Septimus, all they would have had to do was put him under surveillance for seven days and they would have known his every movement throughout the working year.

Septimus rose each morning at seven-fifteen and donned one of his two dark pin-stripe suits. He left his home at 47 Palmerston Drive at seven fifty-five, having consumed his invariable breakfast of one soft-boiled egg, two pieces of toast and two cups of tea. On arriving at Platform One of Sevenoaks station he would purchase a copy of the *Daily Express* before boarding the eight twenty-seven to Cannon Street. During the journey Septimus would read his newspaper and smoke two cigarettes, arriving at Cannon Street at nine-seven. He would then walk to the office, and be sitting at his desk in his glass cubicle on the sixth floor, confronting the first claim to be adjusted, by nine-thirty. He took his coffee break at eleven, allowing himself the luxury of two more cigarettes, when once again he would regale his colleagues with the imagined achievements of his children. At eleven-fifteen he returned to work.

At one o'clock he would leave the Great Gothic Cathedral (another of his expressions) for one hour, which he passed at a pub called The Havelock where he would drink a half-pint of Carlsberg lager with a dash of lime, and eat the dish of the day. After he finished his lunch, he would once again smoke two cigarettes. At one fifty-five he returned to the insurance records until the fifteen-minute tea break at four o'clock, which was another ritual occasion for two more cigarettes. On the dot of five-thirty, Septimus would pick up his umbrella and reinforced steel briefcase with the initials S.H.C. in silver on the side and leave, double locking his glass cubicle. As he walked through the typing pool, he would announce with a mechanical jauntiness, "See you same time tomorrow, girls," hum a few bars from *The Sound of Music* in the descending lift, and then walk out into the torrent of office workers surging down High Holborn. He would stride purposefully toward Cannon Street station, umbrella tapping away on the pavement while he rubbed shoulders with bankers, shippers, oil men and brokers, not discontent to think himself part of the great City of London.

Once he reached the station, Septimus would purchase a copy of the *Evening Standard* and a packet of ten Benson & Hedges cigarettes from Smith's bookstall, placing both on top of his Prudential documents already in the briefcase. He would board the fourth carriage of the train on Platform Five at five-fifty, and secure his favored window seat in a closed compartment facing the engine, next to the balding gentleman with the inevitable *Financial Times*, and opposite the smartly dressed secretary who read long romantic novels to somewhere beyond Sevenoaks. Before sitting down he would extract the *Evening Standard* and the new packet of Benson & Hedges from his briefcase, put them both on the armrest of his seat, and place the briefcase and his rolled umbrella on the rack above him. Once settled, he would open the packet of cigarettes and smoke the first of the two which were allocated for the journey while reading the *Evening Standard*. This would leave him eight to be smoked before catching the five-fifty the following evening.

As the train pulled into Sevenoaks station, he would mumble goodnight to his fellow passengers (the only word he ever spoke during the entire journey) and leave, making his way straight to the semi-detached at 47 Palmerston Drive, arriving at the front door a little before six forty-five. Between six forty-five and seven-thirty he would finish reading his paper or check over his children's homework with a tut-tut when he spotted a mistake, or a sigh when he couldn't fathom the new math. At seven-thirty his "good lady" (another of his favored expressions) would place on the kitchen table in front of him the *Woman's Own* dish of the day or his favorite dinner of three fish fingers, peas and chips. He would then say, "If God had meant fish to have fingers, he would have given them hands," laugh, and cover the oblong fish with tomato sauce, consuming the meal to the accompaniment of his wife's recital of the day's events. At nine, he watched the real news on BBC I (he never watched ITV) and at ten-thirty he retired to bed.

This routine was adhered to year in year out with breaks only for holidays, for which Septimus naturally also had a routine. Alternate Christmases were spent with Norma's parents in Watford and the ones in between with Septimus's sister and brother-in-law in Epsom, while in the summer, their high spot of the year, the family took a package holiday for two weeks in the Olympic Hotel, Corfu.

Septimus not only liked his life-style, but was distressed if for any reason his routine met with the slightest interference. This humdrum existence seemed certain to last him from womb to tomb, for Septimus was not the stuff on which authors base 200,000-word sagas. Nevertheless, there was one occasion when Septimus's routine was not merely interfered with but, frankly, shattered.

One evening at five twenty-seven, when Septimus was closing the file on the last claim for the day, his immediate superior, the Deputy Manager, called him in for a consultation. Owing to this gross lack of consideration, Septimus did not manage to get away from the office until a few minutes after six. Although everyone had left the typing pool, still he saluted the empty desks and silent typewriters with the invariable "See you same time tomorrow, girls," and hummed a few bars of *Edelweiss* to the descending lift. As he stepped out of the Great Gothic Cathedral it started to rain. Septimus reluctantly undid his neatly rolled umbrella and, putting it up, dashed through the puddles, hoping that he would be in time to catch the six thirty-two. On arrival at Cannon Street, he queued for his paper and cigarettes and put them in his briefcase before rushing on to Platform Five. To add to his annoyance, the loudspeaker was announcing with perfunctory apology that three trains had already been taken off that evening because of a go slow.

Septimus eventually fought his way through the dripping, bustling crowds to the sixth carriage of a train that was not scheduled on any timetable. He discovered that it was filled with people he had never seen before and, worse, almost every seat was already occupied. In fact, the only place he could find to sit was in the middle of the train with his back to the engine. He threw his briefcase and creased umbrella onto the rack above him and reluctantly squeezed himself into the seat before looking around the carriage. There was not a familiar face among the other six occupants. A woman with three children more than filled the seat opposite him, while an elderly man was sleeping soundly on his left. On the other side of him, leaning over and looking out of the window, was a young man of about twenty.

When Septimus first laid eyes on the boy he couldn't believe what he saw. The youth was clad in a black leather jacket and skin-tight jeans and was whistling to himself. His dark, creamed hair was combed up at the front and down at the sides, while the only two colors of the young man's outfit that matched were his jacket and fingernails. But worst of all to one of Septimus's sensitive nature was the slogan printed in boot studs on the back of his jacket. "Heil Hitler," it declared unashamedly over a white-painted Nazi sign, and as if that were not enough, below the swastika in gold shone the words: "Up yours." What was the country coming to? thought Septimus. They ought to bring back National Service for delinquents like that. Septimus himself had not been eligible for National Service on account of his flat feet.

Septimus decided to ignore the creature, and picking up the packet of Benson & Hedges on the armrest by his side, lit one and began to read the *Evening Standard*. He then replaced the packet of cigarettes on the armrest, as he always did, knowing he would smoke one more before reaching Sevenoaks. When the train eventually moved out of Cannon Street, the darkly clad youth turned toward Septimus and, glaring at him, picked up the packet of cigarettes, took one, lit it and started to puff away. Septimus could not believe what was happening. He was about to protest when he realized that none of his regulars was in the carriage to back him up. He considered the situation for a moment and decided that discretion was the better part of valor. (Yet another of the sayings of Septimus.)

When the train stopped at Petts Wood, Septimus put down the newspaper although he had scarcely read a word, and as he nearly always did, took his second cigarette. He lit it, inhaled and was about to retrieve the *Evening Standard* when the youth grabbed at the corner, and they ended up with half the paper each. This time Septimus did look around the carriage for support. The children opposite started giggling, while their mother consciously averted her eyes from what was taking place, obviously not wanting to become involved; the old man on Septimus's left was now snoring. Septimus was about to secure the packet of cigarettes by putting them in his pocket when the youth pounced on them, removed another and lit it, inhaled deeply and then blew the smoke quite deliberately across Septimus's face before placing the cigarettes back on the armrest. Septimus's answering glare expressed as much malevolence as he was able to project through the gray haze. Grinding his teeth in fury, he returned to the *Evening Standard*, only to discover that he had ended up with situations vacant, used cars and sports sections, subjects in which he had absolutely no interest. His one compensation, however, was his certainty that sport was the only section the lout really wanted. Septimus was now, in any case, incapable of reading the paper, trembling as he was with the outrages perpetrated by his neighbor.

His thoughts were now turning to revenge and gradually a plan began to form in his mind with which he was confident the youth would be left in no doubt that virtue can sometimes be more than its own reward. (A variation on a saying of Septimus.) He smiled thinly and, breaking his routine, he took a third cigarette and defiantly placed the packet back on the armrest. The youth stubbed out his own cigarette and, as if taking up the challenge, picked up the packet, removed another one and lit it. Septimus was by no means beaten; he puffed his way quickly through the weed, stubbed it out, a quarter unsmoked, took a fourth and lit it immediately. The race was on, for there were now only two cigarettes left. But Septimus, despite a great deal of puffing and coughing, managed to finish his fourth cigarette ahead of the youth. He leaned across the leather jacket and stubbed his cigarette out in the window ashtray. The carriage was now filled with smoke, but the youth was still puffing as fast as he could. The children opposite were coughing and the woman was waving her arms around like a windmill. Septimus ignored her and kept his eye on the packet of cigarettes while pretending to read about Arsenal's chances in the FA cup.

Septimus then recalled Montgomery's maxim that surprise and timing in the final analysis are the weapons of victory. As the youth finished his fourth cigarette and was stubbing it out, the train pulled slowly into Sevenoaks station. The youth's hand was raised, but Septimus was quicker. He had anticipated the enemy's next move, and now seized the cigarette packet. He took out the ninth cigarette and, placing it between his lips, lit it slowly and luxuriously, inhaling as deeply as he could before blowing the smoke out straight into the face of the enemy. The youth stared up at him in dismay. Septimus then removed the last cigarette from the packet and crumpled the tobacco into shreds between his first finger and thumb, allowing the little flakes to fall back into the empty packet. Then he closed the packet neatly, and with a flourish replaced the little gold box on the armrest. In the same movement he picked up from his vacant seat the sports section of the *Evening Standard* and tore the paper in half, in quarters, in eighths and finally in sixteenths, placing the little squares in a neat pile on the youth's lap.

The train came to a halt at Sevenoaks. A triumphant

Septimus, having struck his blow for the silent majority, retrieved his umbrella and briefcase from the rack above him and turned to leave.

As he picked up his briefcase it knocked the armrest in front of him and the lid sprang open. Everyone in the carriage stared at its contents. For there, on top of his Prudential documents, was a neatly folded copy of the *Evening Standard* and an unopened packet of ten Benson & Hedges cigarettes.

One-Night Stand

THE TWO MEN HAD first met at the age of five when they were placed side by side at school, for no more compelling reason than that their names, Thompson and Townsend, came one after the other on the class register. They soon became best friends, a tie which at that age is more binding than any marriage. Having passed their eleven-plus examination they proceeded to the local grammar school with no Timpsons, Tooleys or Tomlinsons to divide them and, after completing seven years in that academic institution, reached an age when one has to go either to work or to university. They opted for the latter on the grounds that work should be put off until the last possible moment. Happily, they both possessed enough brains and native wit to earn themselves places at Durham University to read English.

Undergraduate life turned out to be as sociable as primary school. They both enjoyed English, tennis, cricket, good food and girls. Luckily, in the last of these predilections they differed only on points of detail. Michael, who was six feet two, willowy with dark curly hair, preferred tall, bosomy blondes with blue eyes and long legs. Adrian, a stocky man of five feet ten, with straight, sandy hair, always fell for small, slim, dark-haired, dark-eyed girls. So whenever Adrian came across a girl that Michael took an interest in or vice versa, whether she was an undergraduate or a barmaid, the one would happily exaggerate his friend's virtues. Thus they spent three idyllic years in unison at Durham, gaining considerably more than a Bachelor of Arts degree. As neither of them had impressed the examiners enough to waste a further two years expounding their theories for a Ph.D., they could no longer avoid the real world.

Twin Dick Whittingtons, they set off for London, where Michael joined the BBC as a trainee while Adrian was signed up by Benton and Bowles, the international advertising agency, as an accounts assistant. They acquired a small flat in the Earl's Court Road which they painted orange and brown, and proceeded to live the life of two young blades, for that is undoubtedly how they saw themselves.

Both men spent a further five years in this blissful bachelor state until each fell for a girl who fulfilled his particular requirements. They were married within weeks of each other—Michael to a tall, blue-eyed blonde whom he met while playing tennis at the Hurlingham Club; Adrian to a slim, dark-eyed, dark-haired executive in charge of the Kellogg's Cornflakes account. Each officiated as the other's best man and each proceeded to sire three children at yearly intervals, and in that again they differed, but as before only on points of detail, Michael having two sons and a daughter, Adrian two daughters and a son. Each became godfather to the other's first-born son.

Marriage hardly separated them in anything as they continued to follow much of their old routine, playing cricket together at weekends in the summer and football in the winter, not to mention regular luncheons during the week.

After the celebration of his tenth wedding anniversary, Michael, now a senior producer with Thames Television, admitted rather coyly to Adrian that he had had his first affair: he had been unable to resist a tall, well-built blonde from the typing pool who was offering more than shorthand at seventy words a minute. Only a few weeks later, Adrian, now a senior account manager with Pearl and Dean, also went under, selecting a journalist from Fleet Street who was seeking some inside information on one of the companies he represented. She became a tax-deductible item. After that, the two men quickly fell back into their old routine. Any help they could give each other was provided unstintingly, creating no conflict of interests because of their different tastes. Their married lives were not suffering—or so they convinced each other—and at thirty-five, having come through the swinging sixties unscathed, they began to make the most of the seventies.

Early in that decade, Thames Television decided to send Michael off to America to edit an ABC film about living in New York, for consumption by British viewers. Adrian, who had always wanted to see the eastern seaboard, did not find it hard to arrange a trip at the same time, claiming it was necessary for him to carry out some more than usually spurious research for an Anglo-American tobacco company. The two men enjoyed a lively week together in New York, the highlight of which was a party held by ABC on the final evening to view the edited edition of Michael's film on New York, "An Englishman's View of the Big Apple."

When Michael and Adrian arrived at the ABC studios they found the party already well under way, and both entered the room together, looking forward to a few drinks and an early night before their journey back to England the next day.

They both spotted her at exactly the same moment.

She was of medium height and build, with soft green

eyes and auburn hair—a striking combination of both men's fantasies. Without another thought each knew exactly where he desired to end up that particular night and, two minds with but a single idea, they advanced purposefully upon her.

"Hello, my name is Michael Thompson."

"Hello," she replied. "I'm Debbie Kendall."

"And I'm Adrian Townsend."

She offered her hand and both tried to grab it. When the party had come to an end, they had, between them, discovered that Debbie Kendall was an ABC floor producer on the evening news spot. She was divorced and had two children who lived with her in New York. But neither of them was any nearer to impressing her, if only because each worked so hard to outdo the other; they both showed off abominably and even squabbled over fetching their new companion her food and drink. In the other's absence each found himself running down his closest friend in a subtle but damning way.

"Adrian's a nice chap if it wasn't for his drinking," said Michael.

"Super fellow Michael, such a lovely wife and you should see his three adorable children," added Adrian.

They both escorted Debbie home and reluctantly left her on the doorstep of her 68th Street apartment. She kissed the two of them perfunctorily on the cheek, thanked them and said goodnight. They walked back to their hotel in silence.

When they reached their room on the seventeenth floor of the Plaza, it was Michael who spoke first.

"I'm sorry," he said. "I made a bloody fool of myself."

"I was every bit as bad," said Adrian. "We shouldn't fight over a woman. We never have done in the past."

"Agreed," said Michael. "So why not an honorable compromise?"

"What do you suggest?"

"As we both return to London tomorrow morning, let's agree whichever one of us comes back first . . ."

"Perfect," said Adrian, and they shook hands to seal the bargain, as if they were both back at school playing a cricket match and had to decide on who should bat first. The deal made, they climbed into their respective beds and slept soundly.

Once back in London both men did everything in their power to find an excuse for returning to New York. Neither contacted Debbie Kendall by phone or letter, as it would have broken their gentleman's agreement, but when the weeks grew to be months both become despondent and it seemed that neither was going to be given the opportunity to return. Then Adrian was invited to Los Angeles to address a Media Conference. He remained unbearably smug about the whole trip, confident he would be able to drop into New York on the way back to London. It was Michael who discovered that British Airways were offering cheap tickets for wives who accompanied their husbands on a business trip: Adrian was therefore unable to return via New York. Michael breathed a sigh of relief which turned to triumph when he was selected to go to Washington and cover the President's Address to Congress. He suggested to the head of Outside Broadcasts that it would be wise to drop into New York on the way home and strengthen the contacts he had previously made with ABC. The head of Outside Broadcasts agreed, but told Michael he must be back the following day to cover the opening of Parliament.

Adrian phoned up Michael's wife and briefed her on cheap trips to the States when accompanying your husband. "How kind of you to be so thoughtful, Adrian, but alas my school never allows time off during term, and in any case," she added, "I have a dreadful fear of flying."

Michael was very understanding about his wife's phobia and went off to book a single ticket.

Michael flew into Washington on the following Monday and called Debbie Kendall from his hotel room, wondering if she would even remember the two vainglorious Englishmen she had briefly met some months before, and if she did whether she would also recall which one he was. He dialed nervously and listened to the phone ring. Was she in, was she even in New York? At last a soft voice said hello.

"Hello, Debbie, it's Michael Thompson."

"Hello, Michael. What a nice surprise. Are you in New York?"

"No, Washington, but I'm thinking of flying up. You wouldn't be free for dinner on Thursday by any chance?"

"Let me just check my calendar."

Michael held his breath as he waited. It seemed like hours.

"Yes, that seems to be fine."

"Fantastic. Shall I pick you up around eight?"

"Yes, thank you, Michael. I'll look forward to seeing you then."

Heartened by this early success, Michael immediately penned a telegram of commiseration to Adrian on his sad loss. Adrian didn't reply.

Michael took the shuttle up to New York on Thursday afternoon as soon as he had finished editing the President's speech for the London office. After settling into another hotel room—this time insisting on a double bed just in case Debbie's children were at home—he had a long bath and a slow shave, cutting himself twice and slapping on a little too much aftershave. He rummaged around for his most telling tie, shirt and suit, and after he had finished dressing he studied himself in the mirror, carefully combing his freshly washed hair to make the long thin strands appear casual as well as cover the parts where his hair was beginning to recede. After a final check, he was able to convince himself that he looked less than his thirty-eight years. Michael then took the lift down to the ground floor, and stepping out of the Plaza onto Fifth Avenue he headed jauntily toward 68th Street. En route, he acquired a dozen roses from a little shop at the corner of 65th Street and Madison Avenue and, humming to himself, proceeded confidently. He arrived at the front door of Debbie Kendall's little brownstone at five past eight.

When Debbie opened the door, Michael thought she looked even more beautiful than he had remembered. She was wearing a long blue dress with a frilly white silk collar and cuffs that covered every part of her body from neck to ankles and yet she could not have been more desirable. She wore almost no makeup except a touch of lipstick that Michael already had plans to remove. Her green eyes sparkled.

"Say something," she said, smiling.

"You look quite stunning, Debbie," was all he could think of as he handed her the roses.

"How sweet of you," she replied and invited him in.

Michael followed her into the kitchen, where she cut the long stems and arranged the flowers in a porcelain vase. She then led him into the living room, where she placed the roses on an oval table beside a photograph of two small boys.

"Have we time for a drink?"

"Sure. I've booked a table at Elaine's for eight-thirty."

"My favorite restaurant," she said, with a smile that revealed a small dimple on her cheek. Without asking, Debbie poured two whiskeys and handed one of them to Michael.

What a good memory she has, he thought, as he nervously kept picking up and putting down his glass, like a teenager on his first date. When Michael eventually finished his drink, Debbie suggested that they should leave.

"Elaine wouldn't keep a table free for one minute, even if you were Henry Kissinger."

Michael laughed, and helped her on with her coat. As she unlatched the door, he realized there was no baby-sitter or sound of children. They must be staying with their father, he thought. Once on the street, he hailed a cab and directed the driver to 87th and Second. Michael had never been to Elaine's before. The restaurant had been recommended by a friend from ABC who had assured him: "That joint will give you more than half a chance."

As they entered the crowded room and waited by the bar for the maître d', Michael could see it was the type of place that was frequented by the rich and famous and wondered if his pocket could stand the expense and, more importantly, whether such an outlay would turn out to be a worthwhile investment.

A waiter guided them to a small table at the back of the room, where they both had another whiskey while they studied the menu. When the waiter returned to take their order, Debbie wanted no first course, just the veal piccata, so Michael ordered the same for himself. She refused the addition of garlic butter. Michael allowed his expectations to rise slightly.

"How's Adrian?" she asked.

"Oh, as well as can be expected," Michael replied. "He sends you his love, of course." He emphasized the word love.

"How kind of him to remember me, and please return mine. What brings you to New York this time, Michael? Another film?"

"No. New York may well have become everybody's second city, but this time I only came to see you."

"To see me?"

"Yes, I had a tape to edit while I was in Washington, but I always knew I could be through with that by lunch today so I hoped you would be free to spend an evening with me."

"I'm flattered."

"You shouldn't be."

She smiled. The veal arrived.

"Looks good," said Michael.

"Tastes good, too," said Debbie. "When do you fly home?"

"Tomorrow morning, eleven o'clock flight, I'm afraid."

"Not left yourself time to do much in New York."

"I only came up to see you," Michael repeated. Debbie continued eating her veal. "Why would any man want to divorce you, Debbie?"

"Oh, nothing very original, I'm afraid. He fell in love with a twenty-two year-old blonde and left his thirty-two-year-old wife."

"Silly man. He should have had an affair with the twenty-two-year-old blonde and remained faithful to his thirty-two-year-old wife."

"Isn't that a contradiction in terms?"

"Oh, no, I don't think so. I've never thought it unnatural to desire someone else. After all, it's a long life to go through and be expected never to want another woman."

"I'm not so sure I agree with you," said Debbie thoughtfully. "I would have liked to remain faithful to one man."

Oh hell, thought Michael, not a very auspicious philosophy.

"Do you miss him?" he tried again.

"Yes, sometimes. It's true what they say in the glossy menopause magazines, you can be very lonely when you suddenly find yourself on your own."

That sounds more promising, thought Michael, and he

heard himself saying: "Yes, I can understand that, but someone like you shouldn't have to stay on your own for very long."

Debbie made no reply.

Michael refilled her glass of wine nearly to the brim, hoping he could order a second bottle before she finished her veal.

"Are you trying to get me drunk, Michael?"

"If you think it will help," he replied, laughing.

Debbie didn't laugh. Michael tried again.

"Been to the theater lately?"

"Yes, I went to *Evita* last week. I loved it"—wonder who took you, thought Michael—"but my mother fell asleep in the middle of the second act. I think I shall have to go and see it on my own a second time."

"I only wish I was staying long enough to take you."

"That would be fun," she said.

"Whereas I shall have to be satisfied with seeing the show in London."

"With your wife."

"Another bottle of wine please, waiter."

"No more for me, Michael, really."

"Well, you can help me out a little." The waiter faded away. "Do you get to England at all yourself?" asked Michael.

"No, I've only been once when Roger, my ex, took the whole family. I loved the country. It fulfilled every one of my hopes, but I'm afraid we did what all Americans are expected to do. The Tower of London, Buckingham Palace, followed by Oxford and Stratford, before flying on to Paris."

"A sad way to see England; there's so much more I could have shown you."

"I suspect when the English come to America they don't see much outside of New York, Washington, Los Angeles and perhaps San Francisco."

"I agree," said Michael, not wanting to disagree. The waiter cleared away their empty plates.

"Can I tempt you with a dessert, Debbie?"

"No, no, I'm trying to lose some weight."

Michael slipped a hand gently around her waist. "You don't need to," he said. "You feel just perfect."

She laughed. He smiled.

"Nevertheless, I'll stick to coffee, please."

"A little brandy?"

"No, thank you, just coffee."

"Black?"

"Black."

"Coffee for two, please," Michael said to the hovering waiter.

"I wish I had taken you somewhere a little quieter and less ostentatious," he said, turning back to Debbie.

"Why?"

Michael took her hand. It felt cold. "I would like to have said things to you that shouldn't be listened to by people at the next table."

"I don't think anyone would be shocked by what they overheard at Elaine's, Michael."

"Very well then. Do you believe in love at first sight?"

"No, but I think it's possible to be physically attracted to a person on first meeting them."

"Well, I must confess, I was to you."

Again she made no reply.

The coffee arrived and Debbie released her hand to take a sip. Michael followed suit.

"There were one hundred and fifty women in that room the night we met, Debbie, and my eyes never left you once."

"Even during the film?"

"I'd seen the damn thing a hundred times. I feared I might never see you again."

"I'm touched."

"Why should you be? It must be happening to you all the time."

"Now and then," she said. "But I haven't taken anyone too seriously since my husband left me."

"I'm sorry."

"No need. It's just not that easy to get over someone you've lived with for ten years. I doubt if many divorcees are quite that willing to jump into bed with the first man who comes along as all the latest films suggest."

Michael took her hand again, hoping fervently he did not fall into that category.

"It's been such a lovely evening. Why don't we stroll down to the Carlyle and listen to Bobby Short?" Michael's ABC friend had recommended the move if he felt he was still in with a chance.

"Yes, I'd enjoy that," said Debbie.

Michael called for the bill—eighty-seven dollars. Had it been his wife sitting on the other side of the table he would have checked each item carefully, but not on this occasion. He just left five twenty-dollar bills on a side plate and didn't wait for the change. As they stepped out onto Second Avenue, he took Debbie's hand and together they started walking downtown. On Madison Avenue they stopped in front of shop windows and he bought her a fur coat, a Cartier watch and a Balenciaga dress. Debbie thought it was lucky that all the stores were closed.

They arrived at the Carlyle just in time for the eleven o'clock show. A waiter, flashing a pen light, guided them through the little dark room on the ground floor to a table in the corner. Michael ordered a bottle of champagne as Bobby Short struck up a chord and drawled out the words: "Georgia, Georgia, oh, my sweet . . ." Michael, now unable to speak to Debbie above the noise of the band, satisfied himself with holding her hand and when the entertainer sang, "This time we almost made the pieces fit, didn't we, gal?" he leaned over and kissed her on the cheek. She turned and smiled—was it faintly conspiratorial, or was this just wishful thinking?—and then she sipped her champagne. On the dot of twelve, Bobby Short shut the piano lid and said, "Goodnight, my friends, the time has come for all you good people to go to bed—and some of you naughty ones too." Michael laughed a little too loud but was pleased that Debbie laughed as well.

They strolled down Madison Avenue to 68th Street chatting about inconsequential affairs, while Michael's thoughts were of only one affair. When they arrived at her 68th Street apartment, she took out her latch key.

"Would you like a nightcap?" she asked without any suggestive intonation.

"No more drink, thank you, Debbie, but I would certainly appreciate a coffee."

She led him into the living room.

"The flowers have lasted well," she teased, and left him to make the coffee. Michael amused himself by flicking through an old copy of *Time* magazine, looking at the pictures, not taking in the words. She returned after a few minutes with a coffee pot and two small cups on a lacquered tray. She poured the coffee, black again, and then sat down next to Michael on the couch, drawing one leg underneath her while turning slightly toward him. Michael downed his coffee in two gulps, scalding his mouth slightly. Then, putting down his cup, he leaned over and kissed her on the mouth. She was still clutching her coffee cup. Her eyes opened briefly as she maneuvered the cup onto a side table. After another long kiss she broke away from him.

"I ought to make an early start in the morning."

"So should I," said Michael, "but I am more worried about not seeing you again for a long time."

"What a nice thing to say," Debbie replied.

"No, I just care," he said, before kissing her again.

This time she responded; he slipped one hand onto her breast while the other one began to undo the row of little buttons down the back of her dress. She broke away again.

"Don't let's do anything we'll regret."

"I know we won't regret it," said Michael.

He then kissed her on the neck and shoulders, slipping her dress off as he moved deftly down her body to her breast, delighted to find she wasn't wearing a bra.

"Shall we go upstairs, Debbie? I'm too old to make love on the sofa."

Without speaking, she rose and led him by the hand to her bedroom, which smelled faintly and deliciously of the scent she herself was wearing.

She switched on a small bedside light and took off the rest of her clothes, letting them fall where she stood. Michael never once took his eyes off her body as he undressed clumsily on the other side of the bed. He slipped under the sheets and quickly joined her. When they had finished making love, an experience he hadn't enjoyed as much for a long time, he lay there pondering the fact that she had succumbed at all, especially on their first date.

They lay silently in each other's arms before making love for a second time, which was every bit as delightful as the first. Michael then fell into a deep sleep.

He woke first the next morning and stared across at the beautiful woman who lay by his side. The digital clock on the bedside table showed 7:03. He touched her forehead lightly with his lips and began to stroke her hair. She woke lazily and smiled up at him. Then they made morning love, slowly, gently, but every bit as pleasing as the night before. He didn't speak as she slipped out of bed and ran a bath for him before going to the kitchen to prepare breakfast. Michael relaxed in the hot bath, crooning a Bobby Short number at the top of his voice. How he wished that Adrian could see him now. He dried himself and dressed before joining Debbie in the smart little kitchen where they shared breakfast together. Eggs, bacon, toast, English marmalade and steaming black coffee. Debbie then had a bath and dressed while Michael read the *New York Times*. When she reappeared in the living room wearing a smart coral dress, he was sorry to be leaving so soon.

"We must leave now, or you'll miss your flight."

Michael rose reluctantly and Debbie drove him back to his hotel, where he quickly threw his clothes into a suitcase, settled the bill for his unslept-in double bed and joined her back in the car. On the journey to the airport they chatted about the coming elections and pumpkin pie almost as if they had been married for years or were both avoiding admitting the previous night had ever happened.

Debbie dropped Michael in front of the Pan Am building and put the car in the parking lot before joining him at the check-in counter. They waited for his flight to be called.

"Pan American announces the departure of their Flight Number 006 to London Heathrow. Will all passengers please proceed with their boarding passes to Gate Number Nine."

When they reached the "passengers-only" barrier, Michael took Debbie briefly in his arms. "Thank you for a memorable evening," he said.

"No, it is I who must thank you, Michael," she replied as she kissed him on the cheek.

"I must confess I hadn't thought it would end up quite like that," he said.

"Why not?" she asked.

"Not easy to explain," he replied, searching for words that would flatter and not embarrass. "Let's say I was surprised that . . ."

"You were surprised that we ended up in bed together on our first night? You shouldn't be."

"I shouldn't?"

"No, there's a simple enough explanation. My friends all told me when I got divorced to find myself a man and have a one-night stand. The idea sounded fun but I didn't like the thought of the men in New York thinking I was easy." She touched him gently on the side of his face. "So when I met you and Adrian, both safely living over three thousand miles away, I thought to myself, 'Whichever one of you comes back first . . .' "

Henry's Hiccup

WHEN THE GRAND PASHA'S first son was born in 1900 (he had sired twelve daughters by six wives) he named the boy Henry after his favorite king of England. Henry entered this world with more money than even the most blasé tax collector could imagine and therefore seemed destined to live a life of idle ease.

The Grand Pasha, who ruled over ten thousand families, was of the opinion that in time there would be only five kings left in the world—the kings of spades, hearts, diamonds, clubs and England. With this conviction in mind, he decided that Henry should be educated by the British. The boy was therefore dispatched from his native Cairo at the age of eight to embark upon a formal education, young enough to retain only vague recollections of the noise, the heat and the dirt of his birthplace. Henry started his new life at the Dragon School, which the Grand Pasha's advisers assured him was the finest preparatory school in the land. The boy left this establishment four years later, having developed a passionate love for the polo field and a thorough distaste for the classroom. He proceeded, with the minimum academic qualifications, to

Eton, which the Pasha's advisers assured him was the best school in Europe. He was gratified to learn the school had been founded by his favorite king. Henry spent five years at Eton, where he added squash, golf and tennis to his pastimes, and applied mathematics, jazz and cross-country running to his "avoid at all costs."

On leaving school, he once again failed to make more than a passing impression on the examiners. Nevertheless, he was found a place at Balliol College, Oxford, which the Pasha's advisers assured him was the greatest university in the world. Three years at Balliol added two more loves to his life: horses and women, and three more ineradicable aversions: politics, philosophy and economics.

At the end of his time in *statu pupillari*, he totally failed to impress the examiners and went down without a degree. His father, who considered young Henry's two goals against Cambridge in the Varsity polo match a wholly satisfactory result of his university career, dispatched the boy on a journey round the world to complete his education. Henry enjoyed the experience, learning more on the race course at Longchamps and in the back streets of Benghazi than he ever had acquired from his formal upbringing in England.

The Grand Pasha would have been proud of the tall, sophisticated and handsome young man who returned to England a year later showing only the slightest trace of a foreign accent, if he hadn't died before his beloved son reached Southampton. Henry, although broken-hearted, was certainly not broke, as his father had left him some twenty million in known assets, including a racing stud at Suffolk, a 100-foot yacht in Nice and a palace in Cairo. But by far the most important of his father's bequests was the finest manservant in London, one Godfrey Barker. Barker could arrange or rearrange anything, at a moment's notice.

Henry, for the lack of something better to do, settled himself into his father's old suite at the Ritz, not troubling to read the situations vacant column in the *London Times*. Rather he embarked on a life of single-minded dedication to the pursuit of pleasure, the only career for which Eton, Oxford and inherited wealth had adequately equipped him. To do Henry justice, he had, despite a more than generous helping of charm and good looks, enough common sense to choose carefully those permitted to spend the unforgiving minute with him. He selected only old friends from school and university who, although they were without exception not as well born as he, weren't the sorts of fellows who came begging for the loan of a fiver to cover a gambling debt.

Whenever Henry was asked what was the first love of his life, he was always hard pressed to choose between horses and women, and since he found it possible to spend the day with the one and the night with the other without causing any jealousy or recrimination, he never overtaxed himself with resolving the problem. Most of his horses were fine stallions, fast, sleek, velvet-skinned, with dark eyes and firm limbs; this would have adequately described most of his women, except that they were fillies. Henry fell in and out of love with every girl in the chorus line of the London Palladium, and when the affairs had come to an end, Barker saw to it that they always received some suitable memento to ensure that no scandal ensued. Henry also won every classic race on the English turf before he was thirty-five and Barker always seemed to know the right year to back his master.

Henry's life quickly fell into a routine, never dull. One month was spent in Cairo going through the motions of attending to his business, three months in the south of France with the occasional excursion to Biarritz, and for the remaining eight months he resided at the Ritz. For the four months he was out of London his magnificent suite overlooking St. James's Park remained unoccupied. History does not record whether Henry left the rooms empty because he disliked the thought of unknown persons splashing in the sunken marble bath or because he simply couldn't be bothered with the fuss of signing in and out of the hotel twice a year. The Ritz management had never commented on the matter to his father; why should they with the son? This program fully accounted for Henry's year except for the odd trip to Paris when some home counties girl came a little too close to the altar. Although almost every girl who met Henry wanted to marry him, a good many would have done so even if he had been penniless. However, Henry saw absolutely no reason to be faithful to one woman. "I have a hundred horses and a hundred male friends," he would explain when asked. "Why should I confine myself to one female?" There seemed no immediate answer to Henry's logic.

The story of Henry would have ended there had he continued life as destiny seemed content to allow, but even the Henrys of this world have the occasional hiccup.

As the years passed Henry grew into the habit of never planning ahead, since experience—and his able manservant, Barker—had always led him to believe that with vast wealth you could acquire anything you desired at the last minute, and cover any contingencies that arose later. However, even Barker couldn't formulate a contingency plan in response to Mr. Chamberlain's statement of September 3, 1939, that the British people were at war with Germany. Henry felt it inconsiderate of Chamberlain to have declared war so soon after Wimbledon and the Oaks, and even more inconsiderate of the Home Office to advise him a few months later that Barker must stop serving the Grand Pasha and, until further notice, serve His Majesty the King instead.

What could poor Henry do? Now in his fortieth year, he was not used to living anywhere other than the Ritz, and the Germans who had caused Wimbledon to be canceled were also occupying the George Cinq in Paris and the Negresco in Nice. As the weeks passed and daily an invasion seemed more certain, Henry came to the distasteful conclusion that he would have to return to a neutral Cairo until the British had won the war. It never crossed Henry's mind, even for one moment, that the British might lose. After all, they had won the First World War and therefore they must win the Second. "History repeats itself" was about the only piece of wisdom he recalled clearly from three years of tutorials at Oxford.

Henry summoned the manager of the Ritz and told him that his suite was to be left unoccupied until he returned. He paid one year in advance, which he felt was more than enough time to take care of upstarts like Herr Hitler, and set off for Cairo. The manager was heard to remark later that the Grand Pasha's departure for Egypt was most ironic; he was, after all, more British than the British.

Henry spent a year at his palace in Cairo until he found he could bear his fellow countrymen no longer, so he removed himself to New York only just before it would have been possible for him to come face to face with Rommel. Once in New York, Henry bivouacked in the Pierre Hotel on Fifth Avenue, selected an American manservant called Eugene and waited for Mr. Churchill to finish the war. As if to prove his continuing support for the British, on the first of January every year he forwarded a check to the Ritz to cover the cost of his rooms for the next twelve months.

Henry celebrated V-J Day in Times Square with a million Americans and immediately made plans for his return to Britain. He was surprised and disappointed when the British Embassy in Washington informed him that it might be some time before he was allowed to return to the land he loved, and despite continual pressure and all the influence he could bring to bear, he was unable to board a ship for Southampton until July 1946. From the first-class deck he waved goodbye to America and Eugene, and looked forward to England and Barker.

Once he had stepped off the ship onto English soil he headed straight for the Ritz to find his rooms exactly as he had left them. As far as Henry could see, nothing had changed except that his manservant (now the batman to a general) could not be released from the armed forces for at least another six months. Henry was determined to play his part in the war effort by surviving without him for the ensuing period, and remembering Barker's words: "Everyone knows who you are. Nothing will change," he felt confident all would be well. Indeed on the *Bonheur-du-jour* in his room at the Ritz was an invitation to dine with Lord and Lady Colquhoun in their Chelsea Square home the following night. It looked as if Barker's prediction was turning out to be right: everything would be just the same. Henry penned an affirmative reply to the invitation, happy with the thought that he was going to pick up his life in England exactly where he had left off.

The following evening Henry arrived on the Chelsea Square doorstep a few minutes after eight o'clock. The Colquhouns, an elderly couple who had not qualified for the war in any way, gave every appearance of not even realizing that it had taken place or that Henry had been absent from the London social scene. Their table, despite rationing, was as fine as Henry remembered and, more important, one of the guests present was quite unlike anyone he could ever remember. Her name, Henry learned from his host, was Victoria Campbell, and she turned out to be the daughter of another guest, General Sir Ralph Lympsham. Lady Colquhoun confided to Henry over the quails' eggs that the sad young thing had lost her husband when the allies advanced on Berlin, only a few days before the Germans had surrendered. For the first time Henry felt guilty about not having played some part in the war.

All through dinner, he could not stop staring at young Victoria, whose classical beauty was only equaled by her well-informed and lively conversation. He feared he might be staring too obviously at the slim, dark-haired girl with the high cheekbones; it was like admiring a beautiful sculpture and wanting to touch it. Her bewitching smile elicited an answering smile from all who received it. Henry did everything in his power to be the receiver and was rewarded on several occasions, aware that, for the first time in his life, he was becoming totally infatuated—and was delighted to be.

The ensuing courtship was an unusual one for Henry, in that he made no attempt to persuade Victoria to compliance. He was sympathetic and attentive, and when she had come out of mourning he approached her father and asked if he might request his daughter's hand in marriage. Henry was overjoyed when first the General agreed and later Victoria accepted. After an announcement in *The Times* they celebrated the engagement with a small dinner party at the Ritz, attended by one hundred twenty close friends who might have been forgiven for coming to the conclusion that Attlee was exaggerating about his austerity program. After the last guest had left, Henry walked Victoria back to her father's home in Belgrave Mews, while discussing the wedding arrangements and his plans for the honeymoon.

"Everything must be perfect for you, my angel," he said, as once again he admired the way her long dark hair curled at the shoulders. "We shall be married in St. Margaret's, Westminster, and after a reception at the Ritz we will be driven to Victoria Station, where we will be met by Fred, the senior porter. Fred will allow no one else to carry my bags to the last carriage of the Golden Arrow. One should always have the last carriage, my darling," explained Henry, "so that one cannot be disturbed by other travelers."

Victoria was impressed by Henry's mastery of the arrangements, especially remembering the absence of his manservant, Barker.

Henry warmed to his theme. "Once we have boarded the Golden Arrow, we will be served China tea and some wafer-thin smoked salmon sandwiches which we can enjoy while relaxing on our journey to Dover. When we arrive at the Channel port, we will be met by Albert, whom Fred will have alerted. Albert will remove the bags from our carriage, but not before everyone else has left the train. He will then escort us to the ship, where we will take sherry with the captain while our bags are being placed in cabin number three. Like my father, I always have cabin number three; it is not only the largest and most comfortable stateroom on board, but the cabin is situated in the center of the ship, which makes it possible to enjoy a comfortable crossing even should one have the misfortune to encounter bad weather. And when we have docked in Calais you will find Pierre waiting for us. He will have organized everything for the front carriage of the Flèche d'Or."

"Such a program must take a considerable amount of detailed planning," suggested Victoria, her hazel eyes sparkling as she listened to her future husband's description of the promised tour.

"More tradition than organization I would say, my dear," replied Henry, smiling, as they strolled hand in hand across Hyde Park. "Although, I confess, in the past Barker has kept his eye on things should any untoward emergency arise. In any case I have *always* had the front carriage of the Flèche d'Or because it assures one of being off the train and away before anyone realizes that you have actually arrived in the French capital. Other than Raymond, of course."

"Raymond?"

"Yes, Raymond, a servant *par excellence*, who adored my father; he will have organized a bottle of Veuve Cliquot '37 and a little Russian caviar for the journey. He will also have ensured that there is a couch in the railway carriage should you need to rest, my dear."

"You seem to have thought of everything, Henry darling," she said, as they entered Belgrave Mews.

"I hope you will think so, Victoria; for when we arrive in Paris, which I have not had the opportunity to visit for so many years, there will be a Rolls-Royce standing by the side of the carriage, door open, and we will step out of the Flèche d'Or into the car and Maurice will drive us to the George Cinq, arguably the finest hotel in Europe. Louis, the manager, will be on the steps of the hotel to greet us and he will conduct us to the bridal suite with its stunning view of the city. A maid will unpack for you while you retire to bathe and rest from the tiresome journey. When you are fully recovered we shall dine at Maxim's, where we will be guided to the corner table furthest from the orchestra by Marcel, the finest headwaiter in the world. As we are seated, the musicians will strike up 'A Room with a View,' my favorite tune, and we will then be served the most magnificent langouste you have ever tasted, of that I can assure you."

Henry and Victoria arrived at the front door of the General's small house in Belgrave Mews. He took her hand before continuing.

"After we have dined, my dear, we shall stroll into the Madeleine where I shall buy a dozen red roses from Paulette, the most beautiful flower girl in Paris. She is almost as lovely as you." Henry sighed and concluded: "Then we shall return to the George Cinq and spend our first night together."

Victoria's hazel eyes showed delighted anticipation. "I only wish it could be tomorrow," she said.

Henry kissed her gallantly on the cheek and said: "It will be worth waiting for, my dear. I can assure you it will be a day neither of us will ever forget."

"I'm sure of that," Victoria replied as he released her hand.

On the morning of his wedding Henry leaped out of bed and drew back the curtains with a flourish, only to be greeted by a steady drizzle.

"The rain will clear by eleven o'clock," he said out loud with immense confidence, and hummed as he shaved slowly and with care.

The weather had not improved by mid-morning. On the contrary, heavy rain was falling by the time Victoria entered the church. Henry's disappointment evaporated the instant he saw his beautiful bride; all he could think of was taking her to Paris. The ceremony over, the Grand Pasha and his wife stood outside the church, a golden couple, smiling for the press photographers as the loyal guests scattered damp rice over them. As soon as they decently could, they set off for the reception at the Ritz. Between them they managed to chat to every guest present, and they would have been away in better time had Victoria been a little quicker changing and the General's toast to the happy couple been considerably shorter. The guests crowded onto the steps of the Ritz, overflowing onto the pavement in Piccadilly to wave goodbye to the departing honeymooners, and were only sheltered from the downpour by a capacious red awning.

The General's Rolls took the Grand Pasha and his wife to the station, where the chauffeur unloaded the bags.

Henry instructed him to return to the Ritz now that he had everything under control. The chauffeur touched his cap and said, "I hope you and madam have a wonderful trip, sir," and left them. Henry stood in the station, looking for Fred. There was no sign of him, so he hailed a passing porter.

"Where is Fred?" inquired Henry.

"Fred who?" came the reply.

"How in heaven's name should I know?" said Henry.

"Then how in hell's name should I know?" retorted the porter.

Victoria shivered. English railway stations are not designed for the latest fashion in silk coats.

"Kindly take my bags to the end carriage of the train," said Henry.

The porter looked down at the fourteen bags. "All right," he said reluctantly.

Henry and Victoria stood patiently in the cold as the porter loaded the bags on his trolley and trundled them off along the platform.

"Don't worry, my dear," said Henry. "A cup of Lapsang Souchong tea and some smoked salmon sandwiches and you'll feel a new girl."

"I'm just fine," said Victoria, smiling, though not quite as bewitchingly as usual, as she put her arm through her husband's. They strolled along together to the end carriage.

"Can I check your tickets, sir?" said the conductor, blocking the entrance to the last carriage.

"My what?" said Henry, his accent sounding unusually pronounced.

"Your tic . . . kets," said the conductor, conscious he was addressing a foreigner.

"In the past I have always made the arrangements on the train, my good man."

"Not nowadays you don't, sir. You'll have to go to the booking office and buy your tickets like everyone else, and you'd better be quick about it because the train is due to leave in a few minutes."

Henry stared at the conductor in disbelief. "I assume my wife may rest on the train while I go and purchase the tickets?" he asked.

"No, I'm sorry, sir. No one is allowed to board the train unless they are in possession of a valid ticket."

"Remain here, my dear," said Henry, "and I will deal with this little problem immediately. Kindly direct me to the ticket office, porter."

"End of Platform Four, governor," said the conductor, slamming the train door in annoyance at being described as a porter.

That wasn't quite what Henry had meant by "direct me." Nevertheless, he left his bride with the fourteen bags and somewhat reluctantly headed back toward the ticket office at the end of Platform Four, where he went to the front of a long line.

"There's a queue, you know, mate," someone shouted.

Henry didn't know. "I'm in a frightful hurry," he said.

"And so am I," came back the reply, "so get to the back."

Henry had been told that the British were good at standing in queues, but as he had never had to join one before, he was quite unable to confirm or deny the rumor. He reluctantly walked to the back of the queue. It took some time before Henry reached the front.

"I would like to take the last carriage to Dover."

"You would like what . . .?"

"The last carriage," repeated Henry a little more loudly.

"I am sorry, sir, but every first-class seat is sold."

"I don't want a seat," said Henry. "I require the carriage."

"There are no carriages available nowadays, sir, and as I said, all the seats in first class are sold. I can still fix you up in third class."

"I don't mind what it costs," said Henry. "I must travel first class."

"I don't have a first-class seat, sir. It wouldn't matter if you could afford the whole train."

"I can," said Henry.

"I still don't have a seat left in first class," said the clerk unhelpfully.

Henry would have persisted, but several people in the queue behind him were pointing out that there were only two minutes before the train was due to leave and that they wanted to catch it even if he didn't.

"Two seats then," said Henry, unable to make himself utter the words "third class."

Two green tickets marked Dover were handed through the little grille. Henry took them and started to walk away.

"That will be seventeen and sixpence please, sir."

"Oh, yes, of course," said Henry apologetically. He fumbled in his pocket and unfolded one of the three large white five-pound notes he always carried on him.

"Don't you have anything smaller?"

"No, I do not," said Henry, who found the idea of carrying money vulgar enough without it having to be in small denominations.

The clerk handed back four pounds and a half-crown. Henry did not pick up the half-crown.

"Thank you, sir," said the startled man. It was more than his Saturday bonus.

Henry put the tickets in his pocket and quickly returned to Victoria, who was smiling defiantly against the cold wind; it was not quite the smile that had originally captivated him. Their porter had long ago disappeared and Henry couldn't see another in sight. The conductor took his tickets and clipped them.

"All aboard," he shouted, waved a green flag and blew his whistle.

Henry quickly threw all fourteen bags through the open

door and pushed Victoria onto the moving train before leaping on himself. Once he had caught his breath he walked down the corridor, staring into the third-class carriages. He had never seen one before. The seats were nothing more than thin worn-out cushions, and as he looked into one half-full carriage a young couple jumped in and took the last two adjacent seats. Henry searched frantically for a free carriage but he was unable even to find one with two seats together. Victoria took a single seat in a packed compartment without complaint, while Henry sat forlornly on one of the suitcases in the corridor.

"It will be different once we're in Dover," he said, without his usual self-confidence.

"I am sure it will, Henry," she replied, smiling kindly at him.

The two-hour journey seemed interminable. Passengers of all shapes and sizes squeezed past him in the corridor, treading on his Lobbs hand-made leather shoes, with the words:

"Sorry, sir."

"Sorry, guv."

"Sorry, mate."

Henry put the blame firmly on the shoulders of Clement Attlee and his ridiculous campaign for social equality, and waited for the train to reach Dover Priory Station. The moment the engine pulled in Henry leaped out of the carriage first, not last, and called for Albert at the top of his voice. Nothing happened, except a stampede of people rushed past him on their way to the ship. Eventually Henry spotted a porter and rushed over to him only to find he was already loading up his trolley with someone else's luggage. Henry sprinted to a second man and then on to a third and waved a pound note at a fourth, who came immediately and unloaded the fourteen bags.

"Where to, guv?" asked the porter amicably.

"The ship," said Henry, and returned to claim his bride. He helped Victoria down from the train and they both ran through the rain until, breathless, they reached the gangplank of the ship.

"Tickets, sir," said a young officer in a dark blue uniform at the bottom of the gangplank.

"I always have cabin number three," said Henry between breaths.

"Of course, sir," said the young man and looked at his clipboard. Henry smiled confidently at Victoria.

"Mr. and Mrs. William West."

"I beg your pardon?" said Henry.

"You must be Mr. William West."

"I am certainly not. I am the Grand Pasha of Cairo."

"Well, I'm sorry, sir, cabin number three is booked in the name of a Mr. William West and family."

"I have never been treated by Captain Rogers in this cavalier fashion before," said Henry, his accent now even more pronounced. "Send for him immediately."

"Captain Rogers was killed in the war, sir. Captain Jenkins is now in command of this ship and he never leaves the bridge thirty minutes before sailing."

Henry's exasperation was turning to panic. "Do you have a free cabin?"

The young officer looked down his list. "No, sir, I'm afraid not. The last one was taken a few minutes ago."

"May I have two tickets?" asked Henry.

"Yes, sir," said the young officer. "But you'll have to buy them from the booking office on the quayside."

Henry decided that any further argument would be only time-consuming, so he turned on his heel without another word, leaving his wife with the laden porter. He strode to the booking office.

"Two first-class tickets to Calais," he said firmly.

The man behind the little glass pane gave Henry a tired

look. "It's all one class nowadays, sir, unless you have a cabin."

He proffered two tickets. "That will be one pound exactly."

Henry handed over a pound note, took his tickets, and hurried back to the young officer.

The porter was unloading their suitcases on the quayside.

"Can't you take them on board," cried Henry, "and put them in the hold?"

"No, sir, not now. Only the passengers are allowed on board after the ten-minute signal."

Victoria carried two of the smaller suitcases while Henry humped the twelve remaining ones in relays up the gang-plank. He finally sat down on the deck, exhausted. Every seat seemed already to be occupied. Henry couldn't make up his mind if he was cold from the rain or hot from his exertions. Victoria's smile was fixed firmly in place as she took Henry's hand.

"Don't worry about a thing, darling," she said. "Just relax and enjoy the crossing; it will be such fun being out on deck together."

The ship moved sedately out of the calm of the bay into the Dover Straits. Later that night Captain Jenkins told his wife that the twenty-five-mile journey had been among the most unpleasant crossings he had ever experienced. He added that he had nearly turned back when his second officer, a veteran of two wars, was violently sick. Henry and Victoria spent most of the trip hanging over the rails getting rid of everything they had consumed at their reception. Two people had never been more happy to see land in their life than Henry and Victoria were at the first sight of the Normandy coastline. They staggered off the ship, taking the suitcases one at a time.

"Perhaps France will be different," Henry said lamely, and after a perfunctory search for Pierre he went straight to the booking office and obtained two third-class seats on the Flèche d'Or. They were at least able to sit next to each other this time, but in a carriage already occupied by six other passengers as well as a dog and a hen. The six of them left Henry in no doubt that they enjoyed the modern habit of smoking in public and the ancient custom of taking garlic in their food. He would have been sick again at any other time, but there was nothing left in his stomach. Henry considered walking up and down the train searching for Raymond but feared it could only result in his losing his seat next to Victoria. He gave up trying to hold any conversation with her above the noise of the dog, the hen and the Gallic babble, and satisfied himself by looking out of the window, watching the French countryside and, for the first time in his life, noting the name of every station through which they passed.

Once they arrived at the Gare du Nord, Henry made no attempt to look for Maurice and simply headed straight for the nearest taxi rank. By the time he had transferred all fourteen cases he was well down the queue. He and Victoria stood there for just over an hour, moving the cases forward inch by inch until it was their turn.

"*Monsieur?*"

"Do you speak English?"

"*Un peu, un peu.*"

"Hotel George Cinq."

"*Oui, mais je ne peux pas mettre toutes les valises dans le coffre.*"

So Henry and Victoria sat huddled in the back of the taxi, bruised, tired, soaked and starving, surrounded by leather suitcases, only to be bumped up and down over the cobble stones all the way to the George Cinq.

The hotel doorman rushed to help them as Henry offered the taxi driver a pound note.

"No take English money, *monsieur.*"

Henry couldn't believe his ears. The doorman happily paid the taxi driver in francs and quickly pocketed the pound note. Henry was too tired even to comment. He helped Victoria up the marble steps and went over to the reception desk.

"The Grand Pasha of Cairo and his wife. The bridal suite, please."

"*Oui, monsieur.*"

Henry smiled at Victoria.

"You 'ave your booking confirmation with you?"

"No," said Henry, "I have never needed to confirm my booking with you in the past. Before the war I . . ."

"I am sorry, sir, but the 'otel is fully booked at the moment. A conference."

"Even the bridal suite?" asked Victoria.

"Yes, Madam, the chairman and his lady, you understand." He nearly winked.

Henry certainly did not understand. There had always been a room for him at the George Cinq whenever he had wanted one in the past. Desperate, he unfolded the second of his five-pound notes and slipped it across the counter.

"Ah," said the booking clerk, "I see we still have one room unoccupied, but I fear it is not very large."

Henry waved a listless hand.

The booking clerk banged the bell on the counter in front of him with the palm of his hand, and a porter appeared immediately and escorted them to the promised room. The booking clerk had been telling the truth. Henry could only have described the room they found themselves standing in as a box. The reason that the curtains were perpetually drawn was that the view over the chimneys of Paris was singularly unprepossessing, but that was not to be the final blow, as Henry realized, staring in disbelief at the sight of the two narrow single beds. Victoria started unpacking without a word while Henry sat despondently on the end of one of them. After Victoria had sat soaking in a bath that was the perfect size for a six-year-old, she lay down exhausted on the other bed. Neither spoke for nearly an hour.

"Come on, darling," said Henry finally. "Let's go and have dinner."

Victoria rose loyally but reluctantly and dressed for dinner while Henry sat in the bath, knees on nose, trying to wash himself before changing into evening dress. This time he phoned the front desk and ordered a taxi as well as booking a table at Maxim's.

The taxi driver did accept his pound note on this occasion, but as Henry and his bride entered the great restaurant he recognized no one and no one recognized him. A waiter led them to a small table hemmed in between two other couples just below the band. As he walked into the dining room the musicians struck up "Alexander's Ragtime Band."

They both ordered from the extensive menu and the langouste turned out to be excellent, every bit as good as Henry had promised of Maxim's, but by then neither of them had the stomach to eat a full meal and the greater part of both their dishes was left on the plate.

Henry found it hard to convince the new headwaiter that the lobster had been superb and that they had purposely come to Maxim's not to eat it. Over coffee, he took Victoria's hand and tried to apologize.

"Let us end this farce," he said, "by completing my plan and going to the Madeleine and presenting you with the promised flowers. Paulette will not be in the square to greet you but there will surely be someone who can sell us roses."

Henry called for the bill and unfolded the third five-pound note (Maxim's is always happy to accept other people's currency and certainly didn't bother him with any change) and they left, walking hand in hand toward the Madeleine. For once Henry turned out to be right, for Paulette was nowhere to be seen. An old lady with a shawl over her head and a wart on the side of her nose stood in her place on the corner of the square, surrounded by the most beautiful flowers.

Henry selected a dozen of the longest-stemmed red roses and then placed them in the arms of his bride. The old lady smiled at Victoria.

Victoria returned her smile.

"*Dix francs, monsieur*," said the old lady to Henry.

Henry fumbled in his pocket, only to discover he had spent all his money. He looked despairingly at the old lady, who raised her hands, smiled at him and said:

"Don't worry, Henry, have them on me. For old times' sake."

A Matter of Principle

SIR HAMISH GRAHAM HAD many of the qualities and most of the failings that result from being born to a middle-class Scottish family. He was well educated, hard-working and honest, while at the same time being narrow-minded, uncompromising and proud. Never on any occasion had he allowed hard liquor to pass his lips, and he mistrusted all men who had not been born north of Hadrian's Wall, and many of those who had.

After spending his formative years at Fettes School, to which he had won a minor scholarship, and at Edinburgh University, where he obtained a second-class honors degree in engineering, he was chosen from a field of twelve to be a trainee with the international construction company TarMac (named after its founder, J. L. McAdam, who discovered that tar when mixed with stones was the best constituent for making roads). The new trainee, through diligent work and uncompromising tactics, became the firm's youngest and most disliked project manager. By the age of thirty Graham had been appointed deputy managing director of TarMac and was already beginning to realize that he could not hope to progress much farther while he was in someone else's employ. He therefore began to think of forming his own company. When two years later the chairman of TarMac, Sir Alfred Hickman, offered Graham the opportunity to replace the retiring managing director, he resigned immediately. After all, if Sir Alfred felt he had the ability to run TarMac he must also be competent enough to start his own company.

The next day, young Hamish Graham made an appointment to see the local manager of the Bank of Scotland who was responsible for the TarMac account, and with whom he had dealt for the past ten years. Graham explained to the manager his plans for the future, submitting a full written proposal, and requesting that his overdraft facility be extended from fifty pounds to ten thousand. Three weeks later Graham learned that his application had been viewed favorably. He remained in his lodgings in Edinburgh, while renting an office in the north of the city (or, to be more accurate, a room at ten shillings a week). He purchased a typewriter, hired a secretary and ordered some unembossed headed letter-paper. After a further month of diligent interviewing, he employed two engineers, both graduates of Aberdeen University, and five out-of-work laborers from Glasgow.

During those first few weeks on his own Graham tendered for several small road contracts in the central lowlands of Scotland, the first seven of which he failed to secure. Preparing a tender is always time-consuming and often expensive, so by the end of his first six months in business Graham was beginning to wonder if his sudden departure from TarMac had not been foolhardy. For the first time in his life he experienced self-doubt, but that was soon removed by the Ayrshire County Council, who accepted his tender to construct a minor road which was to join a projected school with the main highway. The road was only five hundred yards in length, but the assignment took

Graham's little team seven months to complete and when all the bills had been paid and all expenses taken into account Graham Construction made a net loss of £143.10s.6d.

Still, in the profit column was a small reputation which had been invisibly earned, and caused the Ayrshire Council to invite him to build the school at the end of their new road. This contract made Graham Construction a profit of £420 and added still further to his reputation. From that moment Graham Construction went from strength to strength, and as early as his third year in business he was able to declare a small pre-tax profit, and this grew steadily over the next five years. When Graham Construction was floated on the London Stock Exchange the demand for the shares was over-subscribed ten times and the newly quoted company was soon considered a blue-chip institution, a considerable achievement for Graham to have pulled off in his own lifetime. But then the City likes men who grow slowly and can be relied on not to involve themselves in unnecessary risks.

In the sixties Graham Construction built motorways, hospitals, factories and even a power station, but the achievement the chairman took most pride in was Edinburgh's newly completed art gallery, which was the only contract that showed a deficit in the annual general report. The invisible earnings column, however, recorded the award of knight bachelor for the chairman.

Sir Hamish decided that the time had come for Graham Construction to expand into new fields, and looked, as generations of Scots had before him, toward the natural market of the British Empire. He built in Australia and Canada with his own finances, and in India and Africa with a subsidy from the British government. In 1963 he was named "Businessman of the Year" by *The Times* and three years later "Chairman of the Year" by *The Econo-*

mist. Sir Hamish never once altered his methods to keep pace with the changing times, and if anything grew more stubborn in the belief that his ideas of doing business were correct whatever anyone else thought; and he had a long credit column to prove he was right.

In the early seventies, when the slump hit the construction business, Graham Construction suffered the same cut in budgets and lost contracts as any of its major competitors. Sir Hamish reacted in a predictable way, by tightening his belt and paring his estimates while at the same time refusing one jot to compromise his business principles. The company therefore grew leaner and many of his more enterprising young executives left Graham Construction for firms which still believed in taking on the occasional risky contract.

Only when the slope of the profits graph started taking on the look of a downhill slalom did Sir Hamish become worried. One night, while brooding over the company's profit-and-loss account for the previous three years, and realizing that he was losing contracts even in his native Scotland, Sir Hamish reluctantly came to the conclusion that he must tender for less established work, and perhaps even consider the odd gamble.

His brightest young executive, David Heath, a stocky, middle-aged bachelor, whom he did not entirely trust—after all, the man had been educated south of the border and worse, at some extraordinary place in the United States called the Wharton Business School—wanted Sir Hamish to put a toe into Mexican waters. Mexico, as Heath was not slow to point out, had discovered vast reserves of oil off its eastern coast and had overnight become rich with American dollars. The construction business in Mexico was suddenly proving most lucrative and contracts were coming up for tender with figures as high as thirty to forty million dollars attached to them.

Heath urged Sir Hamish to go after one such contract that had recently been announced in a full-page advertisement in *The Economist*. The Mexican government was issuing tender documents for a proposed ring road around its capital, Mexico City. In an article in the business section of *The Observer*, detailed arguments were put forward as to why established British companies should try to fulfill the ring road tender. Heath had offered shrewd advice on overseas contracts in the past that Sir Hamish had subsequently let slip through his fingers.

The next morning, Sir Hamish sat at his desk listening attentively to David Heath, who felt that because Graham Construction had already built the Glasgow and Edinburgh ring roads any application they made to the Mexican government had to be taken seriously. To Heath's surprise, Sir Hamish agreed with his project manager and allowed a team of six men to travel to Mexico to obtain the tender documents and research the project.

The research team was led by David Heath, and consisted of three other engineers, a geologist and an accountant. When the team arrived in Mexico they obtained the tender documents from the Minister of Works and settled down to study them minutely. Having pinpointed the major problems, they walked around Mexico City with their ears open and their mouths shut and made a list of the problems they were clearly going to encounter: the impossibility of unloading anything at Vera Cruz and then transporting the cargo to Mexico City without half of the original assignment being stolen, the lack of communications between ministries, and worst of all the attitude of the Mexicans to the dictionary definition of work. But David Heath's most positive contribution to the list was to discover that each minister had his own outside man, and that man had better be well disposed to Graham Construction if the firm were to be even considered for the short list. Heath immediately sought out the Minister of Works man, one Victor Perez, and took him to an extravagant lunch at the Fonda el Refugio, where both of them nearly ended up drunk, although Heath remained sober enough to agree on all of the necessary terms, conditional upon Sir Hamish's approval. Having taken every possible precaution, Heath agreed with Perez on a tender figure which was to include the minister's percentage. Once he had completed the report for his chairman, he flew back to England with his team.

On the evening of David Heath's return, Sir Hamish retired to bed early to study his project manager's conclusions. He read the report through the night as others might read a spy story, and was left in no doubt that this was the opportunity he had been looking for to overcome the temporary setbacks Graham Construction was now suffering. Although Sir Hamish would be up against Costains, Sunleys and John Brown, as well as many international companies, he still felt confident that any application he made must have a "fair chance." On arrival at his office the next morning Sir Hamish sent for David Heath, who was delighted by the chairman's initial response to his report.

Sir Hamish started speaking as soon as his burly project manager entered the room, not even inviting him to take a seat.

"You must contact our Embassy in Mexico City immediately and inform them of our intentions," pronounced Sir Hamish. "I may speak to the Ambassador myself," he said, intending that to be the concluding remark of the interview.

"Useless," said David Heath.

"I beg your pardon?"

"I don't wish to appear rude, sir, but it doesn't work like that any more. Britain is no longer a great power dispensing largesse to all far-flung and grateful recipients."

"More's the pity," said Sir Hamish.

The project manager continued as though he had not heard his chairman.

"The Mexicans now have vast wealth of their own and the United States, Japan, France and Germany keep massive embassies in Mexico City with highly professional trade delegations trying to influence every ministry."

"But surely history counts for something," said Sir Hamish. "Wouldn't they rather deal with an established British company than some upstarts from—?"

"Perhaps, sir, but in the end all that really matters is which minister is in charge of what contract and who is his outside representative."

Sir Hamish looked puzzled. "Your meaning is obscure to me, Mr. Heath."

"Allow me to explain, sir. Under the present system in Mexico, each ministry has an allocation of money to spend on projects agreed to by the government. Every Secretary of State is acutely aware that his tenure of office may be very short, so he picks out a major contract for himself from the many available. It's the one way to ensure a pension for life if the government is changed overnight or the minister simply loses his job."

"Don't bandy words with me, Mr. Heath. What you are suggesting is that I should bribe a government official. I have never been involved in that sort of thing in thirty years of business."

"And I wouldn't want you to start now," replied Heath. "The Mexicans are far too experienced in business etiquette for anything as clumsy as that to be suggested, but while the law requires that you appoint a Mexican agent, it must make sense to try and sign up the minister's man, who in the end is the one person who can ensure that you will be awarded the contract. The system seems to work well, and as long as a minister deals only with reputable international firms and doesn't become greedy, no one complains. Fail to observe either of those two golden rules and the whole house of cards collapses. The minister ends up in Le Cumberri for thirty years and the company concerned has all its assets expropriated and is banned from any future business dealings in Mexico."

"I really cannot become involved in such shenanigans," said Sir Hamish. "I still have my shareholders to consider."

"*You* don't have to become involved," Heath rejoined. "After we have tendered for the contract you wait and see if the company has been shortlisted and then, if we have, you wait again to find out if the minister's man approaches us. I know the man, so if he does make contact we have a deal. After all, Graham Construction is a respectable international company."

"Precisely, and that's why it's against my principles," said Sir Hamish with hauteur.

"I do hope, Sir Hamish, it's also against your principles to allow the Germans and the Americans to steal the contract from under our noses."

Sir Hamish glared back at his project manager but remained silent.

"And I feel I must add, sir," said David Heath, moving restlessly from foot to foot, "that the pickings in Scotland haven't exactly yielded a harvest lately."

"All right, all right, go ahead," said Sir Hamish reluctantly. "Put in a tender figure for the Mexico City ring road and be warned if I find bribery is involved, on your head be it," he added, banging his closed fist on the table.

"What tender figure have you settled on, sir?" asked the project manager. "I believe, as I stressed in my report, that we should keep the amount under forty million dollars."

"Agreed," said Sir Hamish, who paused for a moment

and smiled to himself before saying: "Make it $39,121,110."

"Why that particular figure, sir?"

"Sentimental reasons," said Sir Hamish, without further explanation.

David Heath left, pleased that he had convinced his boss to go ahead, but he feared it might in the end prove harder to overcome Sir Hamish's principles than the entire Mexican government. Nevertheless he filled in the bottom line of the tender as instructed and then had the document signed by three directors including his chairman, as required by Mexican law. He sent the tender by special messenger to be delivered at the Ministry of Buildings in Paseo de la Reforma: when tendering for a contract for over thirty-nine million dollars, one does not send the document by first-class post.

Several weeks passed before the Mexican Embassy in London contacted Sir Hamish, requesting that he travel to Mexico City for a meeting with Manuel Unichurtu, the minister concerned with the city's ring road project. Sir Hamish remained skeptical, but David Heath was jubilant, because he had already learned through another source that Graham Construction was the only tender being seriously considered at that moment, although there were one or two outstanding items still to be agreed on. David Heath knew exactly what that meant.

A week later Sir Hamish, traveling first class, and David Heath, traveling economy, flew out of Heathrow bound for Mexico's international airport. On arrival they took an hour to clear customs and another thirty minutes to find a taxi to take them to the city, and then only after the driver had bargained with them for an outrageous fare. They covered the fifteen-mile journey from the airport to their hotel in just over an hour and Sir Hamish was able to observe at first hand why the Mexicans were so desperate to build a ring road. Even with the windows down, the ten-year-old car was like an oven that had been left on high all night, but during the journey Sir Hamish never once loosened his collar or tie. The two men checked into their rooms, phoned the minister's secretary to inform her of their arrival, and then waited.

For two days, nothing happened.

David Heath assured his chairman that such a hold-up was not an unusual course of events in Mexico, as the minister was undoubtedly in meetings most of the day, and after all wasn't "*mañana*" the one Spanish word every foreigner understood?

On the afternoon of the third day, only just before Sir Hamish was threatening to return home, David Heath received a call from the minister's man, who accepted an invitation to join them both for dinner in Sir Hamish's suite that evening.

Sir Hamish put on evening dress for the occasion, despite David Heath's counseling against the idea. He even had a bottle of Fina La Ina sherry sent up in case the minister's man required some refreshment. The dinner table was set and the hosts were ready for seven-thirty. The minister's man did not appear at seven-thirty, or seven forty-five, or eight o'clock or eight-fifteen, or eight-thirty. At eight forty-nine there was a loud rap on the door, and Sir Hamish muttered an inaudible reproach as David Heath went to open it and find his contact standing there.

"Good evening, Mr. Heath, I'm sorry to be late. Held up with the minister, you understand."

"Yes, of course," said David Heath. "How good of you to come, Señor Perez. May I introduce my chairman, Sir Hamish Graham?"

"How do you do, Sir Hamish? Victor Perez at your service."

Sir Hamish was dumbfounded. He simply stood and stared at the little middle-aged Mexican who had arrived for dinner dressed in a grubby white T-shirt and Western jeans. Perez looked as if he hadn't shaved for three days and reminded Sir Hamish of those bandits he had seen in B-movies when he was a schoolboy. He wore a heavy gold bracelet around his wrist that could have come from Cartier's and a tiger's tooth on a platinum chain around his neck that looked as if it had come from Woolworth's. Perez grinned from ear to ear, pleased with the effect he was having on the chairman of Graham Construction.

"Good evening," replied Sir Hamish stiffly, taking a step backward. "Would you care for a sherry?"

"No, thank you, Sir Hamish. I've grown into the habit of liking your whisky, on the rocks with a little soda."

"I'm sorry, I only have . . ."

"Don't worry, sir, I have some in my room," said David Heath, and rushed away to retrieve a bottle of Johnnie Walker he had hidden under the shirts in his top drawer. Despite this Scottish aid, the conversation before dinner among the three men was somewhat stilted, but David Heath had not come five thousand miles for an inferior hotel meal with Victor Perez, and Victor Perez in any other circumstances would not have crossed the road to meet Sir Hamish Graham even if he'd built it. Their conversation ranged from the recent visit to Mexico of Her Majesty the Queen—as Sir Hamish referred to her—to the proposed return trip of President Portillo to Britain. Dinner might have gone more smoothly if Mr. Perez hadn't eaten most of the food with his hands and then proceeded to clean his fingers on the side of his jeans. The more Sir Hamish stared at him in disbelief the more the little Mexican would grin from ear to ear. After dinner David Heath thought the time had come to steer the conversation toward the real purpose of the meeting, but not before Sir Hamish had reluctantly had to call for a bottle of brandy and a box of cigars.

"We are looking for an agent to represent the Graham Construction Company in Mexico, Mr. Perez, and you have been highly recommended," said Sir Hamish, sounding unconvinced by his own statement.

"Do call me Victor."

Sir Hamish bowed silently and shuddered. There was no way this man was going to be allowed to call him Hamish.

"I'd be pleased to represent you, Hamish," continued Perez, "provided that you find my terms acceptable."

"Perhaps you could enlighten us as to what those—hm, terms—might be," said Sir Hamish stiffly.

"Certainly," said the little Mexican cheerfully. "I require ten percent of the agreed tender figure, five percent to be paid on the day you are awarded the contract and five percent whenever you present your completion certificates. Not a penny to be paid until you have received your fee, all my payments deposited in an account at Credit Suisse in Geneva within seven days of the National Bank of Mexico clearing your check."

David Heath drew in his breath sharply and stared down at the stone floor.

"But under those terms you would make nearly four million dollars," protested Sir Hamish, now red in the face. "That's over half our projected profit."

"That, as I believe you say in England, Hamish, is your problem. You fixed the tender price," said Perez, "not me. In any case, there's still enough in the deal for both of us to make a handsome profit, which is surely fair as we both bring half the equation to the table."

Sir Hamish was speechless as he fiddled with his bow tie. David Heath examined his fingernails attentively.

"Think the whole thing over, Hamish," said Victor Perez, sounding unperturbed, "and let me know your decision by midday tomorrow. The outcome makes little difference to me." The Mexican rose, shook hands with Sir Hamish and left. David Heath, sweating slightly, accompanied him down in the lift. In the foyer he clasped hands damply with the Mexican.

"Good night, Victor. I'm sure everything will be all right—by midday tomorrow."

"I hope so," replied the Mexican, "for your sake." He strolled out of the foyer whistling.

Sir Hamish, a glass of water in his hand, was still seated at the dinner table when his project manager returned.

"I do not believe it is possible that that—that that man can represent the Secretary of State, represent a government minister."

"I am assured that he does," replied David Heath.

"But to part with nearly four million dollars to such an individual . . ."

"I agree with you, sir, but that is the way business is conducted out here."

"I can't believe it," said Sir Hamish. "I *won't* believe it. I want you to make an appointment for me to see the minister first thing tomorrow morning."

"He won't like that, sir. It might expose his position, and put him right out in the open in a way that could only embarrass him."

"I don't give a damn about embarrassing him. We are discussing a bribe, do I have to spell it out for you, Heath? A bribe of nearly four million dollars. Have you no principles, man?"

"Yes, sir, but I would still advise you against seeing the Secretary of State. He won't want any of your conversation with Mr. Perez on the record."

"I have run this company my way for nearly thirty years, Mr. Heath, and I shall be the judge of what I want on the record."

"Yes, or course, sir."

"I will see the Secretary of State first thing in the morning. Kindly arrange a meeting."

"If you insist, sir," said David Heath resignedly.

"I insist."

The project manager departed to his own room and a sleepless night. Early the next morning he delivered a handwritten, personal and private letter to the minister, who sent a car round immediately for the Scottish industrialist.

Sir Hamish was driven slowly through the noisy, exuberant, bustling crowds of the city in the minister's black Ford Galaxy with the flag flying. People made way for the car respectfully. The chauffeur came to a halt outside the Ministry of Buildings and Public Works in Paseo de la Reforma and guided Sir Hamish through the long white corridors to a waiting room. A few minutes later an assistant showed Sir Hamish through to the Secretary of State and took a seat by his side. The minister, a severe-looking man who appeared to be well into his seventies, was dressed in an immaculate white suit, white shirt and blue tie. He rose, leaned over the vast expanse of green leather and offered his hand.

"Do have a seat, Sir Hamish."

"Thank you," the chairman said, feeling more at home as he took in the minister's office; on the ceiling a large propellor-like fan revolved slowly, making little difference to the stuffiness of the room, while hanging on the wall behind the minister was a signed picture of President José López Portillo in full morning dress and below the photo a plaque displaying a coat of arms.

"I see you were educated at Cambridge."

"That is correct, Sir Hamish, I was up at Corpus Christi College for three years."

"Then you know my country well, sir."

"I do have many happy memories of my stays in

England, Sir Hamish; in fact, I still visit London as often as my leave allows."

"You must take a trip to Edinburgh some time."

"I have already done so, Sir Hamish. I attended the Festival on two occasions and now know why your city is described as the Athens of the North."

"You are well informed, Minister."

"Thank you, Sir Hamish. Now I must ask how I can help you. Your assistant's note was rather vague."

"First let me say, Minister, that my company is honored to be considered for the city ring road project and I hope that our experience of thirty years in construction, twenty of them in the third world"—he nearly said the undeveloped countries, an expression his project manager had warned him against—"is the reason you, as minister in charge, found us the natural choice for this contract."

"That, and your reputation for finishing a job on time at the stipulated price," replied the Secretary of State. "Only twice in your history have you returned to the principal asking for changes in the payment schedule. Once in Uganda when you were held up by Amin's pathetic demands, and the other project, if I remember rightly, was in Bolivia, an airport, when you were unavoidably delayed for six months because of an earthquake. In both cases, you completed the contract at the new price stipulated and my principal advisers think you must have lost money on both occasions." The Secretary of State mopped his brow with a silk handkerchief before continuing. "I would not wish you to think my government takes these decisions of selection lightly."

Sir Hamish was astounded by the Secretary of State's command of his brief, the more so as no prompting notes lay on the leather-topped desk in front of him. He suddenly felt guilty at the little he knew about the Secretary of State's background or history.

"Of course not, Minister. I am flattered by your personal

concern, which makes me all the more determined to broach an embarrassing subject that has . . ."

"Before you say anything else, Sir Hamish, may I ask you some questions?"

"Of course, Minister."

"Do you still find the tender price of $39,121,110 acceptable in *all* the circumstances?"

"Yes, Minister."

"That amount still leaves you enough to do a worthwhile job while making a profit for your company?"

"Yes, Minister, but . . ."

"Excellent, then I think all you have to decide is whether you want to sign the contract by midday today." The minister emphasized the word "midday" as clearly as he could.

Sir Hamish, who had never understood the expression "a nod is as good as a wink," charged foolishly on.

"There is, nevertheless, one aspect of the contract I feel that I should discuss with you privately."

"Are you sure that would be wise, Sir Hamish?"

Sir Hamish hesitated, but only for a moment, before proceeding. Had David Heath heard the conversation that had taken place so far, he would have stood up, shaken hands with the Secretary of State, removed the top of his fountain pen and headed toward the contract—but not his employer.

"Yes, Minister, I feel I must," said Sir Hamish firmly.

"Will you kindly leave us, Miss Vieites?" said the Secretary of State.

The assistant closed her shorthand book, rose and left the room. Sir Hamish waited for the door to close before he began again.

"Yesterday I had a visit from a countryman of yours, a Mr. Victor Perez, who resides here in Mexico City and claims—"

"An excellent man," said the minister very quietly.

Still Sir Hamish charged on. "Yes, I daresay he is, Minister, but he asked to be allowed to represent Graham Construction as our agent and I wondered—"

"A common practice in Mexico, no more than is required by the law," said the minister, swinging his chair around and staring out of the window.

"Yes, I appreciate that is the custom," said Sir Hamish, now talking to the minister's back, "but if I am to part with ten percent of the government's money I must be convinced that such a decision meets with your personal approval." Sir Hamish thought he had worded that rather well.

"Um," said the Secretary of State, measuring his words, "Victor Perez is a good man and has always been loyal to the Mexican cause. Perhaps he leaves an unfortunate impression sometimes, not out of what you would call the 'top drawer,' Sir Hamish, but then we have no class barriers in Mexico." The minister swung back to face Sir Hamish.

The Scottish industrialist flushed. "Of course not, Minister, but that, if you will forgive me, is hardly the point. Mr. Perez is asking me to hand over nearly four million dollars, which is over half of my estimated profit on the project, without allowing for any contingencies or mishaps that might occur later."

"You chose the tender figure, Sir Hamish. I confess I was amused by the fact you added your date of birth to the thirty-nine million."

Sir Hamish's mouth opened wide.

"I would have thought," continued the minister, "given your record over the past three years and the present situation in Britain, you were not in a position to be fussy."

The minister gazed impassively at Sir Hamish's startled face. Both started to speak at the same time. Sir Hamish swallowed his words.

"Allow me to tell you a little story about Victor Perez.

When the war was at its fiercest" (the old Secretary of State was referring to the Mexican Revolution, in the same way that an American thinks of Vietnam or a Briton of Germany when they hear the word "war"), "Victor's father was one of the young men under my command who died on the battlefield at Celaya only a few days before victory was ours. He left a son born on the day of independence who never knew his father. I have the honor, Sir Hamish, to be godfather to that child. We christened him Victor."

"I can understand that you have a responsibility to an old comrade, but I still feel four million is—"

"Do you? Then let me continue. Just before Victor's father died I visited him in a field hospital and he asked only that I should take care of his wife. She died in childbirth. I therefore considered my responsibility passed on to their only child."

Sir Hamish remained silent for a moment. "I appreciate your attitude, Minister, but ten percent of one of your largest contracts?"

"One day," continued the Secretary of State, as if he had not heard Sir Hamish's comment, "Victor's father was fighting in the front line at Zacatecas and looking out across a minefield he saw a young lieutenant, lying face down in the mud with his leg nearly blown off. With no thought for his own safety, he crawled through that minefield until he reached the lieutenant and then he dragged him yard by yard back to the camp. It took him over three hours. He then carried the lieutenant to a truck and drove him to the nearest field hospital, undoubtedly saving his leg, and probably his life. So you see the government has good cause to allow Perez's son the privilege of representing it from time to time."

"I agree with you, Minister," said Sir Hamish quietly. "Quite admirable." The Secretary of State smiled for the first time. "But I still confess I cannot understand why you allow him such a large percentage."

The minister frowned. "I am afraid, Sir Hamish, if you cannot understand that, you can never hope to understand the principles we Mexicans live by."

The Secretary of State rose from behind his desk, limped to the door and showed Sir Hamish out.

The Hungarian Professor

COINCIDENCES, AUTHORS ARE TOLD (usually by the critics), must be avoided, although in truth the real world is full of incidents that in themselves are unbelievable. Everyone has had an experience that, if they wrote about it, would appear to others to be pure fiction.

The same week that the headlines in the world newspapers read "Russia Invades Afghanistan," "America to Withdraw from Moscow Olympics" there also appeared a short obituary in *The Times* for the distinguished Professor of English at the University of Budapest. "A man who was born and died in his nation's capitol and whose reputation remains assured by his brilliant translation of the works of Shakespeare into his native Hungarian. Although some linguists consider his *Coriolanus* immature they universally acknowledge his *Hamlet* to be a translation of genius."

Nearly a decade after the Hungarian Revolution I had the chance to participate in a student athletics meeting in Budapest. The competition was scheduled to last for a full week, so I felt there would be an opportunity to find out a little about the country. The team flew in to Ferihegy Airport on Sunday night and we were taken immediately to the Hotel Ifushag. (I learned later that the word meant youth in Hungarian.) Having settled in, most of the team went to bed early since their opening round heats were the following day.

Breakfast the next morning consisted of milk, toast and an egg, served in three acts with long intervals between them. Those of us who were running that afternoon skipped lunch for fear that a matinee performance might cause us to miss our events completely.

Two hours before the start of the meeting, we were taken by bus to the Nép stadium and unloaded outside the dressing rooms (I have always felt they should be called undressing rooms). We changed into track suits and sat around on benches anxiously waiting to be called. After what seemed to be an interminable time but was in fact only a few minutes, an official appeared and led us out onto the track. Because it was the opening day of competition, the stadium was packed. When I had finished my usual warm-up of jogging, sprinting and some light calisthenics, the loudspeaker announced the start of the 100-meter race in three languages. I stripped off my track suit and ran over to the start. When called, I pressed my spikes against the blocks and waited nervously for the starter's pistol. Felkészülni, Kész—bang. Ten seconds later the race was over and the only virtue of coming in last was that it left me six free days to investigate the Hungarian capital.

Walking around Budapest reminded me of my childhood days in Bristol just after the war, but with one noticeable difference. In addition to the bombed-out buildings, there was row upon row of bullet holes in some of the walls. The revolution, although eight years past, was still much in evidence, perhaps because the nationals did not want anyone to forget. The people on the streets had lined faces, stripped of all emotion, and they shuffled rather than walked, leaving the impression of a nation of old men. If you inquired innocently why, they told you there was nothing to hurry for, or to be happy about, although they always seemed to be thoughtful with each other.

On the third day of the games, I returned to the Nép stadium to support a friend of mine who was competing in the semi-finals of the 400-meter hurdles, the first event that afternoon. Having a competitor's pass, I could sit virtually anywhere in the half-empty arena. I chose to watch the race from just above the final bend, giving me a good view of the home straight. I sat down on the wooden bench without paying much attention to the people on either side of me. The race began and as my friend hit the bend crossing the seventh hurdle with only three hurdles to cover before the finishing line, I stood and cheered him heartily all the way down the home straight. He managed to come in third, ensuring himself a place in the final the following day. I sat down again and wrote out the detailed result in my program. I was about to leave, as there were no British competitors in the hammer or the pole vault, when a voice behind me said:

"You are English?"

"Yes," I replied, turning in the direction from which the question had been put.

An elderly gentleman looked up at me. He wore a three-piece suit that must have been out of date when his father owned it, and even lacked the possible virtue that some day the style might come back into fashion. The leather patches on the elbows left me in no doubt that my questioner was a bachelor, for they could only have been sewn on by a man—either that or one had to conclude he had elbows in odd places. The length of his trousers revealed that his father had been two inches taller than he. As for the man himself, he had a few strands of white hair, a walrus mustache and ruddy cheeks. His tired blue eyes were perpetually half-closed, like the shutter of a camera that has just been released. His forehead was so lined that he might have been any age between fifty and seventy. The overall impression was of a cross between a tram inspector and an out-of-work violinist.

I sat down for a second time.

"I hope you didn't mind my asking?" he added.

"Of course not," I said.

"It's just that I have so little opportunity to converse with an Englishman. So when I spot one I always grasp the nettle. Is that the right colloquial expression?"

"Yes," I said, trying to think how many Hungarian words I knew. Yes, No, Good morning, Goodbye, I am lost, Help.

"You are in the student games?"

"Were, not are," I said. "I departed somewhat rapidly on Monday."

"Because you were not rapid enough, perhaps?"

I laughed, again admiring his command of my first language.

"Why is your English so excellent?" I inquired.

"I'm afraid it's a little neglected," the old man replied. "But they still allow me to teach the subject at the university. I must confess to you that I have absolutely no interest in sport, but these occasions always afford me the opportunity to capture someone like yourself and oil the rusty machine, even if only for a few minutes." He gave me a tired smile but his eyes were now alight.

"What part of England do you hail from?" For the first time his pronunciation faltered as "hail" came out as "heel."

"Somerset," I told him.

"Ah," he said, "perhaps the most beautiful county in England." I smiled, as most foreigners never seem to travel much beyond Oxford or Stratford-on-Avon. "To drive across the Mendips," he continued, "through perpetually green hilly countryside and to stop at Cheddar to see Gough's caves, at Wells to be amused by the black swans ringing the bell on the Cathedral wall, or at Bath to admire the life-style of classical Rome, and then perhaps to go over the county border and on to Devon . . . Is Devon even more beautiful than Somerset, in your opinion?"

"Never," said I.

"Perhaps you are a little prejudiced," he laughed. "Now let me see if I can recall:

> Of the western counties there are seven
> But the most glorious is surely Devon.

Perhaps Hardy, like you, was prejudiced and could think only of his beloved Exmoor, the village of Tiverton and Drake's Plymouth."

"Which is *your* favorite county?" I asked.

"The North Riding of Yorkshire has always been underrated, in my opinion," replied the old man. "When people talk of Yorkshire, I suspect Leeds, Sheffield and Barnsley spring to mind. Coal mining and heavy industry. Visitors should travel and see the dales there; they will find them as different as chalk from cheese. Lincolnshire is too flat and so much of the Midlands must now be spoiled by sprawling towns. The Birminghams of this world hold no appeal for me. But in the end I come down in favor of Worcestershire and Warwickshire, quaint old English villages nestling in the Cotswolds and crowned by Stratford-upon-Avon. How I wish I could have been in England in 1959 while my countrymen were recovering from the scars of revolution. Olivier performing Coriolanus, another man who did not want to show his scars."

"I saw the performance," I said. "I went with a school party."

"Lucky boy. I translated the play into Hungarian at the age of nineteen. Reading over my work again last year made me aware I must repeat the exercise before I die."

"You have translated other Shakespeare plays?"

"All but three. I have been leaving *Hamlet* to last, and then I shall return to *Coriolanus* and start again. As you are a student, am I permitted to ask which university you attend?"

"Oxford."

"And your college?"

"Brasenose."

"Ah. B.N.C. How wonderful to be a few yards away from the Bodleian, the greatest library in the world. If I had been born in England I should have wanted to spend my days at All Souls, that is just opposite B.N.C., is it not?"

"That's right."

The professor stopped talking while we watched the next race, the first semi-final of the 1,500 meters. The winner was Anfras Patovich, a Hungarian, and the partisan crowd went wild with delight.

"That's what I call support," I said.

"Like Manchester United when they have scored the winning goal in the Cup Final. But my fellow countrymen do not cheer because the Hungarian was first," said the old man.

"No?" I said, somewhat surprised.

"Oh, no, they cheer because he beat the Russian."

"I hadn't even noticed," I said.

"There is no reason why you should, but their presence is always in the forefront of our minds and we are rarely given the opportunity to see them beaten in public."

I tried to steer him back to a happier subject. "And

before you had been elected to All Souls, which college would you have wanted to attend?"

"As an undergraduate, you mean?"

"Yes."

"Undoubtedly Magdalen is the most beautiful college. It has the distinct advantage of being situated on the River Cherwell; and in any case I confess a weakness for perpendicular architecture and a love of Oscar Wilde." The conversation was interrupted by the sound of a pistol and we watched the second semi-final of the 1,500 meters, which was won by Orentas of the U.S.S.R., and the crowd showed its disapproval more obviously this time, clapping in such a way that left hands passed by right without coming into contact. I found myself joining in on the side of the Hungarians. The scene made the old man lapse into a sad silence. The last race of the day was won by Tim Johnston of England and I stood and cheered unashamedly. The Hungarian crowd clapped politely.

I turned to say goodbye to the professor, who had not spoken for some time.

"How long are you staying in Budapest?" he asked.

"The rest of the week. I return to England on Sunday."

"Could you spare the time to join an old man for dinner one night?"

"I should be delighted."

"How considerate of you," he said, and he wrote out his full name and address in capital letters on the back of my program and returned it to me. "Why don't we say tomorrow at seven? And if you have any old newspapers or magazines do bring them with you," he said, looking a little sheepish. "And I shall quite understand if you have to change your plans."

I spent the next morning looking over St. Matthias Church and the ancient fortress, two of the buildings that showed no evidence of the revolution. I then took a short trip down the Danube before spending the afternoon supporting the swimmers at the Olympic pool. At six I left the pool and went back to my hotel. I changed into my team blazer and gray slacks, hoping I looked smart enough for my distinguished host. I locked my door and started toward the lift and then remembered. I returned to my room to pick up the pile of newspapers and magazines I had collected from the rest of the team.

Finding the professor's home was not as easy as I had expected. After meandering around cobbled streets and waving the professor's address at several passers-by, I was finally directed to an old apartment block. I ran up the three flights of the wooden staircase in a few leaps and bounds, wondering how long the climb took the professor every day. I stopped at the door that displayed his number and knocked.

The old man answered immediately, as if he had been standing there, waiting by the door. I noticed that he was wearing the same suit he had had on the previous day.

"I am sorry to be late," I said.

"No matter, my own students also find me hard to find the first time," he said, grasping my hand. He paused. "Bad to use the same word twice in the same sentence. 'Locate' would have been better, wouldn't it?"

He trotted on ahead of me, not waiting for my reply, a man obviously used to living on his own. He led me down a small dark corridor into his drawing room. I was shocked by its small size. Three sides were covered with indifferent prints and watercolors depicting English scenes, while the fourth wall was dominated by a large bookcase. I could spot Shakespeare, Dickens, Austen, Trollope, Hardy, even Waugh and Graham Greene. On the table was a faded copy of the *New Statesman*. I looked around to see if we were alone, but there seemed to be no sign of a wife or child either in person or picture, and indeed the table was only set for two.

The old man turned and stared with childish delight at my pile of newspapers and magazines.

"*Punch, Time* and the *Observer*, a veritable feast," he declared, gathering them into his arms before placing them lovingly on his bed in the corner of the room.

The professor then opened a bottle of Szürkebarát and left me to look at the pictures while he prepared the meal. He slipped away into an alcove which was so small that I had not realized the room contained a kitchenette. He continued to bombard me with questions about England, many of which I was quite unable to answer.

A few minutes later he stepped back into the room, requesting me to take a seat. "Do be seated," he said, on reflection. "I do not wish you to remove the seat. I wish you to sit on it." He put a plate in front of me which had on it a leg of something that might have been a chicken, a piece of salami and a tomato. I felt sad, not because the food was inadequate, but because he believed it to be plentiful.

After dinner, which despite my efforts to eat slowly and hold him in conversation, did not take up much time, the old man made some coffee, which tasted bitter, and then filled a pipe before we continued our discussion. We talked of A. L. Rowse and his views on Shakespeare and then he turned to politics.

"Is it true," the professor asked, "that England will soon have a Labor government?"

"The opinion polls seem to indicate as much," I said.

"I suppose the British feel that Sir Alec Douglas-Home is not swinging enough for the sixties," said the professor, now puffing vigorously away at his pipe. He paused and looked up at me through the smoke. "I did not offer you a pipe, because I assumed after your premature exit in the first round of the competition you would not be smoking." I smiled. "But Sir Alec," he continued, "is a man with long experience in politics and it's no bad thing for a country to be governed by an experienced gentleman."

I would have laughed out loud had the same opinion been expressed by my own tutor.

"And what of the Labor leader?" I said, forbearing to mention his name.

"Molded in the white heat of a technological revolution," he replied. "I am not so certain. I liked Gaitskell, an intelligent and shrewd man. An untimely death. Attlee, like Sir Alec, was a gentleman. But as for Mr. Wilson, I suspect that history will test his mettle—a pun which I had not intended—in that white heat and only then will we discover the truth."

I could think of no reply.

"I was considering last night after we parted," the old man continued, "the effect that Suez must have had on a nation which only ten years before had won a world war. The Americans should have backed you. Now we read in retrospect, always the historian's privilege, that at the time Prime Minister Eden was tired and ill. The truth was he didn't receive the support from his closest allies when he most needed it."

"Perhaps we should have supported you in 1956."

"No, no, it was too late then for the West to shoulder Hungary's problems. Churchill understood that in 1945. He wanted to advance beyond Berlin and to free all the nations that bordered Russia. But the West had had a bellyful of war by then and left Stalin to take advantage of that apathy. When Churchill coined the phrase 'the Iron Curtain,' he foresaw exactly what was going to happen in the East. Amazing to think that when that great man said 'if the British Empire should last a thousand years,' it was in fact destined to survive for only twenty-five. How I wish he had still been around the corridors of power in 1956."

"Did the revolution greatly affect your life?"

"I do not complain. It is a privilege to be the Professor of English in a great university. They do not interfere with me in my department and Shakespeare is not yet considered subversive literature." He paused and took a luxuriant puff at his pipe. "And what will you do, young man, when you leave the university—as you have shown us that you cannot hope to make a living as a runner?"

"I want to be a writer."

"Then travel, travel, travel," he said. "You cannot hope to learn everything from books. You must see the world for yourself if you ever hope to paint a picture for others."

I looked up at the old clock on his mantelpiece only to realize how quickly the time had passed.

"I must leave you, I'm afraid; they expect us all to be back in the hotel by ten."

"Of course," he said, smiling, "the English public school mentality. I will accompany you to Kossuth Square and then you will be able to see your hotel on the hill."

As we left the flat, I noticed that he didn't bother to lock the door. Life had left him little to lose. He led me quickly through the myriad of narrow roads that I had found so impossible to navigate earlier in the evening, chatting about this building and that, an endless fund of knowledge about his own country as well as mine. When we reached Kossuth Square he took my hand and held it, as lonely people often will, reluctant to let go.

"Thank you for allowing an old man to indulge himself by chattering on about his favorite subject."

"Thank you for your hospitality," I said, "and when you are next in Somerset you must come to Lympsham and meet my family."

"Lympsham? I cannot place it," he said, looking worried.

"I'm not surprised. The village has a population of only twenty-two."

"Enough for two cricket teams," remarked the professor. "A game, I confess, with which I have never come to grips."

"Don't worry," I said, "neither have half the English."

"Ah, but I should like to. What is a gully, a no-ball, a night watchman? The terms have often intrigued me."

"Then remember to get in touch when you're next in England and I'll take you to Lord's and see if I can teach you something."

"How kind," he said, and then he hesitated before adding: "But I don't think we shall meet again."

"Why not?" I asked.

"Well, you see, I have never been outside Hungary in my whole life. When I was young I couldn't afford to, and now I don't imagine that those in authority would allow me to see your beloved England."

He released my hand, turned and shuffled back into the shadows of the side streets of Budapest.

I read his obituary in *The Times* once again as well as the headlines about Afghanistan and its effect on the Moscow Olympics.

He was right. We never met again.

The First Miracle

TOMORROW IT WOULD BE I A.D, but nobody had told him.

If anyone had, he wouldn't have understood, because he thought that it was the forty-third year in the reign of the Emperor, and in any case, he had other things on his mind. His mother was still cross with him and he had to admit that he'd been naughty that day, even by the standards of a normal thirteen-year-old. He hadn't meant to drop the pitcher when she had sent him to the well for water. He tried to explain to his mother that it wasn't his fault that he had tripped over a stone; and that at least was true. What he hadn't told her was that he was chasing a stray dog at the time. And then there was that pomegranate; how was he meant to know that it was the last one, and that his father had taken a liking to them? The boy was now dreading his father's return and the possibility that he might be given another thrashing. He could still remember the last one, when he hadn't been able to sit down for two days without feeling the pain, and the thin red scars didn't completely disappear for more than three weeks.

He sat on the window ledge in a shaded corner of his room trying to think of some way he could redeem himself in his mother's eyes, now that she had thrown him out of the kitchen. Go outside and play, she had insisted, after he had spilled some cooking oil on his tunic. But that wasn't much fun, because he was only allowed to play by himself. His father had forbidden him to mix with the local boys. How he hated this country; if only he were back home with his friends, there would be so much to do. Still, only another three weeks and he could . . . The door swung open and his mother came into the room. She was dressed in the thin black garments so favored by locals: they kept her cool, she had explained to the boy's father. He had grunted his disapproval, so she always changed back into imperial dress before he returned in the evening.

"Ah, there you are," she said, addressing the crouched figure of her son.

"Yes, Mother."

"Daydreaming as usual. Well, wake up because I need you to go into the village and fetch some food for me."

"Yes, Mother, I'll go at once," the boy said as he jumped off the window ledge.

"Well, at least wait until you've heard what I want."

"Sorry, Mother."

"Now listen, and listen carefully." She started counting on her fingers as she spoke. "I need a chicken, some raisins, figs, dates and . . . ah yes, two pomegranates."

The boy's face reddened at the mention of the pomegranates and he stared down at the stone floor, hoping she might have forgotten. His mother put her hand into the leather purse that hung from her waist and removed two small coins, but before she handed them over she made her son repeat the instructions.

"One chicken, raisins, figs, dates and two pomegranates," he recited, as he might the modern poet, Virgil.

"And be sure to see they give you the correct change," she added. "Never forget the locals are all thieves."

"Yes, Mother . . ." For a moment the boy hesitated.

"If you remember everything and bring back the right amount of money, I might forget to tell your father about the broken pitcher and the pomegranate."

The boy smiled, pocketed the two small silver coins in his tunic and ran out of the house into the compound. The centurion who stood on duty at the gate removed the great wedge of wood, which allowed the massive door to swing open. The boy jumped through the hole in the gate and grinned back at the young officer.

"Been in more trouble again today?" the guard shouted after him.

"No, not this time," the boy replied. "I'm about to be saved."

He waved farewell to the guard and started to walk briskly toward the village while humming a tune that reminded him of home. He kept to the center of the dusty winding path that the locals had the nerve to call a road. He seemed to spend half his time removing little stones from his sandals. If his father had been posted here for any length of time he would have made some changes; then they would have had a real road, straight and wide enough to take a chariot. But not before his mother had sorted out the serving girls. Not one of them knew how to lay a table or even prepare food so that it was at least clean. For the first time in his life he had seen his mother in a kitchen, and he felt sure it would be the last, as they would all be returning home now that his father was coming to the end of his assignment.

The evening sun shone down on him as he walked; it was a very large red sun, the same red as his father's tunic. The heat it gave out made him sweat and long for something to drink. Perhaps there would be enough money left over to buy himself a pomegranate. He couldn't wait to take one home and show his friends how large they were in this barbaric land. Marcus, his best friend, would undoubtedly have seen one as big because his father had commanded a whole army in these parts, but the rest of the class would still be impressed.

The village to which his mother had sent him was only two miles from the compound and the dusty path ran alongside a hill overlooking a large valley. The road was already crowded with travelers who would be seeking shelter in the village. All of them had come down from the hills at the express orders of his father, whose authority had been vested in him by the Emperor himself. Once he was sixteen, he too would serve the Emperor. His friend Marcus wanted to be a soldier and conquer the rest of the world. But he was more interested in the law and teaching his country's customs to the heathens in strange lands.

Marcus had said, "I'll conquer them and then you can govern them."

A sensible division between brains and brawn, he had told his friend, who didn't seem impressed and had ducked him in the nearest bath.

The boy quickened his pace, for he knew he had to be back in the compound before the sun disappeared behind the hills. His father had told him many times that he must always be locked safely inside before sunset. He was aware that his father was not a popular man with the locals, and he had warned his son that he would always be safe while it was light since no one would dare to harm him while others could watch what was going on, but once it was dark anything could happen. One thing he knew for certain: when he grew up he wasn't going to be a tax collector or work in the census office.

When he reached the village he found the narrow twisting lanes that ran between the little white houses swarming with people who had come from all the neighboring lands to obey his father's order and be registered for the census, in order that they might be taxed. The boy dismissed the plebs from his mind. (It was Marcus who had taught him to refer to all foreigners as plebs.) When he entered the marketplace he also dismissed Marcus from his mind and began to concentrate on the supplies his mother wanted. He mustn't make any mistakes this time or he would undoubtedly end up with that thrashing from his father. He ran nimbly between the stalls, checking the food carefully. Some of the local people stared at the fair-skinned boy with the curly brown hair and the straight, firm nose. He displayed no imperfections or disease like the majority of them. Others turned their eyes away from him; after all, he had come from the land of the natural rulers. These thoughts did not pass through his mind. All the boy noticed was that their native skins were parched and lined from too much sun. He knew that too much sun was bad for you: it made you old before your time, his tutor had warned him.

At the end stall the boy watched an old woman haggling over an unusually plump live chicken, and as he marched toward her she ran away in fright, leaving the fowl behind her. He stared at the stallkeeper and refused to bargain with the peasant. It was beneath his dignity. He pointed to the chicken and gave the man one denarius. The man bit the round silver coin and looked at the head of Augustus Caesar, ruler of half the world. (When his tutor had told him, during a history lesson, about the Emperor's achievements, he remembered thinking, I hope Caesar doesn't conquer the whole world before I have a chance to join in.) The stallkeeper was still staring at the silver coin.

"Come on, come on, I haven't got all day," said the boy, imitating his father.

The local did not reply because he couldn't understand what the boy was saying. All he knew for certain was that it would be unwise for him to annoy the invader. The stallkeeper held the chicken firmly by the neck and, taking a knife from his belt, cut its head off in one movement and passed the dead fowl over to the boy. He then handed back some of his local coins, which had stamped on them the image of a man the boy's father described as "that useless Herod." The boy kept his hand held out, palm open, and the local placed bronze talents into it until he had no more. The boy left him talentless and moved to another stall, this time pointing to bags containing raisins, figs and dates. The new stallkeeper made a measure of each, for which he received five of the useless Herod coins. The man was about to protest about the barter, but the boy stared at him fixedly in the eyes, the way he had seen his father do so often. The stallkeeper backed away and only bowed his head.

Now, what else did his mother want? He racked his brains. A chicken, raisins, dates, figs and . . . of course, two pomegranates. He searched among the fresh-fruit stalls and picked out three pomegranates, and breaking one open, began to eat it, discarding the rind on the ground in front of him. He paid the stallkeeper with the two remaining bronze talents, feeling pleased that he had carried out his mother's wishes while still being able to return home with one of the silver denarii. Even his father would be impressed by that. He finished the pomegranate and, with his arms laden, headed slowly out of the market back toward the compound, trying to avoid the stray dogs that continually got under his feet. They barked and sometimes snapped at his ankles: they did not know who he was.

When the boy reached the edge of the village he noticed the sun was already disappearing behind the highest hill, so he quickened his pace, remembering his father's words about being home before dusk. As he walked down the stony path, those still on the way toward the village kept a respectful distance, leaving him a clear vision as far as the eye could see, which wasn't all that far since he was carrying so much in his arms. But one sight he did notice a little way ahead of him was a man with a beard—a dirty, lazy habit, his father had told him—wearing the ragged dress that signified that he was of the tribe of Jacob, tugging a reluctant donkey which in turn was carrying a very fat woman. The woman was, as their custom demanded, covered from head to toe in black. The boy was about to order them out of his path when the man left the donkey on the side of the road and went into a house which, from its sign, claimed to be an inn.

Such a building in his own land would never have passed the scrutiny of the local councilors as a place fit for paying travelers to dwell in. But the boy realized that this particular week to find even a mat to lay one's head on might be considered a luxury. He watched the bearded man reappear through the door with a forlorn look on his tired face. There was clearly no room at the inn.

The boy could have told him that before he went in, and wondered what the man would do next, since it was the last dwelling house on the road. Not that he was really interested; they could both sleep in the hills for all he cared. It was about all they looked fit for. The man with the beard was telling the woman something and pointing behind the inn, and without another word he led the donkey off in the direction he had been indicating. The boy wondered what could possibly be at the back of the inn and, his curiosity roused, followed them. As he came to the corner of the building, he saw that the man was coaxing the donkey through an open door of what looked like a barn. The boy followed the strange trio and watched them through the crack left by the open door. The barn was covered in dirty straw and full of chickens, sheep and oxen, and smelled to the boy like the sewers they built in the side streets back home. He began to feel sick. The man was clearing away some of the worst of the straw from the center of the barn, trying to make a clean patch for them to rest on—a near hopeless task, thought the boy. When the man had done as best he could he lifted the fat woman down from the donkey and placed her gently in the straw. Then he left her and went over to a trough on the other side of the barn where one of the oxen was drinking. He cupped his fingers together, put them in the trough and, filling his hands with water, returned to the fat woman.

The boy was beginning to get bored and was about to leave when the woman leaned forward to drink from the man's hands. The shawl fell from her head and he saw her face for the first time.

He stood transfixed, staring at her. He had never seen anyone more beautiful. Unlike the common members of her tribe, the woman's skin was translucent in quality, and her eyes shone, but what most struck the boy was her manner and presence. Never had he felt so much in awe, even remembering his one visit to the Senate House to hear a declamation from Augustus Caesar.

For a moment he remained mesmerized, but then he knew what he must do. He walked through the open door toward the woman, fell on his knees before her and offered the chicken. She smiled and he gave her the pomegranates and she smiled again. He then dropped the rest of the food in front of her, but she remained silent. The man with the beard was returning with more water, and when he saw the young foreigner he fell on his knees, spilling the water onto the straw, and then covered his face. The boy stayed on his knees for some time before he rose and walked slowly toward the barn door. When he reached the opening, he turned back and stared once more into the face of the beautiful woman. She still did not speak.

The young Roman hesitated only for a second, and then bowed his head.

It was already dusk when he ran back out onto the

winding path to resume his journey home, but he was not afraid. Rather he felt he had done something good and therefore no harm could come to him. He looked up into the sky and saw directly above him the first star, shining so brightly in the east that he wondered why he could see no others. His father had told him that different stars were visible in different lands, so he dismissed the puzzle from his mind, replacing it with the anxiety of not being home before dark. The road in front of him was now empty, so he was able to walk quickly toward the compound, and was not all that far from safety when he first heard the singing and shouting. He turned quickly to see where the danger was coming from, staring up into the hills above him. To begin with, he couldn't make sense of what he saw. Then his eyes focused in disbelief on one particular field in which the shepherds were leaping up and down, singing, shouting and clapping their hands. The boy noticed that all the sheep were safely penned in a corner of the field for the night, so they had nothing to fear. He had been told by Marcus that sometimes the shepherds in this land would make a lot of noise at night because they believed it kept away the evil spirits. How could anyone be that stupid, the boy wondered, when there was a flash of lightning across the sky and the field was suddenly ablaze with light. The shepherds fell to their knees, silent, staring up into the sky for several minutes as though they were listening intently to something. Then all was darkness again.

The boy started running toward the compound as fast as his legs could carry him; he wanted to be inside and hear the safety of the great gate close behind him and watch the centurion put the wooden wedge firmly back in its place. He would have run all the way had he not seen something in front of him that brought him to a sudden halt. His father had taught him never to show any fear when facing danger. The boy caught his breath in case it would make them think that he was frightened. He was frightened, but he marched proudly on, determined he would never be forced off the road. When they did meet face to face, he was amazed.

Before him stood three camels and astride the beasts three men, who stared down at him. The first was clad in gold and with one arm protected something hidden beneath his cloak. By his side hung a large sword, its sheath covered in all manner of rare stones, some of which the boy could not even name. The second was dressed in white and held a silver casket to his breast, while the third wore red and carried a large wooden box. The man robed in gold put up his hand and addressed the boy in a strange tongue which he had never heard uttered before, even by his tutor. The second man tried Hebrew but to no avail and the third yet another tongue without eliciting any response from the boy.

The boy folded his arms across his chest and told them who he was and where he was going, and asked where they might be bound. He hoped his piping voice did not reveal his fear. The one robed in gold replied first and questioned the boy in his own tongue.

"Where is he that is born King of the Jews? For we have seen his star in the east, and are come to worship him."

"King Herod lives beyond the . . ."

"We speak not of King Herod," said the second man, "for he is but a king of men as we are."

"We speak," said the third, "of the King of Kings and are come to offer him gifts of gold, frankincense and myrrh."

"I know nothing of the King of Kings," said the boy, now gaining in confidence. "I recognize only Augustus Caesar, Emperor of the known world."

The man robed in gold shook his head and, pointing to the sky, inquired of the boy: "You observe that bright star in the east. What is the name of the village on which it shines?"

The boy looked up at the star, and indeed the village below was clearer to the eye than it had been in sunlight.

"But that's only Bethlehem," said the boy, laughing. "You will find no King of Kings there."

"Even there we shall find him," said the second king, "for did not Herod's chief priest tell us:

> And thou Bethlehem, in the land of Judah,
> Art not least among the princes of Judah,
> For out of thee shall come a Governor
> That shall rule my people Israel."

"It cannot be," said the boy, now almost shouting at them. "Augustus Caesar rules Israel and all the known world."

But the three robed men did not heed his words and left him to ride on toward Bethlehem.

Mystified, the boy set out on the last part of his journey home. Although the sky had become pitch black, whenever he turned his eyes toward Bethlehem the village was still clearly visible in the brilliant starlight. Once again he started running toward the compound, relieved to see its outline rising up in front of him. When he reached the great wooden gate, he banged loudly and repeatedly until a centurion, sword drawn, holding a flaming torch, came out to discover who it was that disturbed his watch. When he saw the boy, he frowned.

"Your father is very angry. He returned at sunset and is about to send out a search party for you."

The boy darted past the centurion and ran all the way to his family's quarters, where he found his father addressing a sergeant of the guard. His mother was standing by his side, weeping.

The father turned when he saw his son and shouted: "Where have you been?"

"To Bethlehem."

"Yes, I know that, but whatever possessed you to return so late? Have I not told you countless times never to be out of the compound after dark? Come to my study at once."

The boy looked helplessly toward his mother, who was still crying, but now out of relief, and turned to follow his father into the study. The guard sergeant winked at him as he passed by, but the boy knew nothing could save him now. His father strode ahead of him into the study and sat on a leather stool by his table. His mother followed and stood silently by the door.

"Now tell me exactly where you have been and why you took so long to return, and be sure to tell me the truth."

The boy stood in front of his father and told him everything that had come to pass. He started with how he had gone to the village and taken great care in choosing the food and in so doing had saved half the money his mother had given him. How on the way back he had seen a fat lady on a donkey unable to find a place at the inn, and then he explained why he had given her the food. He went on to describe how the shepherds had shouted and beat their breasts until there was a great light in the sky at which they had all fallen silent on their knees, and then finally how he had met the three robed men who were searching for the King of Kings.

The father grew angry at his son's words.

"What a story you tell," he shouted. "Do tell me more. Did you find this King of Kings?"

"No, sir. I did not," he replied, as he watched his father rise and start pacing around the room.

"Perhaps there is a more simple explanation of why

your face and fingers are stained red with pomegranate juice," he suggested.

"No, Father. I did buy an extra pomegranate, but even after I had bought all the food, I still managed to save one silver denarius."

The boy handed the coin over to his mother, believing it would confirm his story. But the sight of the piece of silver only made his father more angry. He stopped pacing and stared down into the eyes of his son.

"You have spent the other denarius on yourself and now you have nothing to show for it?"

"That's not true, Father, I . . ."

"Then I will allow you one more chance to tell me the truth," said his father as he sat back down. "Fail me, boy, and I shall give you a thrashing that you will never forget for the rest of your life."

"I have already told you the truth, Father."

"Listen to me carefully, my son. We were born Romans, born to rule the world because our laws and customs are tried and trusted and have always been based firmly on absolute honesty. Romans never lie; it remains our strength and the weakness of our enemies. That is why we rule while others are ruled and as long as that is so the Roman Empire will never fall. Do you understand what I am saying, my boy?"

"Yes, Father, I understand."

"Then you'll also understand why it is imperative to tell the truth."

"But I have not lied, Father."

"Then there is no hope for you," said the man angrily. "And you leave me only one way to deal with this matter."

The boy's mother wanted to come to her son's aid, but knew any protest would be useless. The father rose from his chair and removed the leather belt from around his waist and folded it double, leaving the heavy brass studs on the outside. He then ordered his son to touch his toes. The young boy obeyed without hesitation and the father raised the leather strap above his head and brought it down on the child with all his strength. The boy never flinched or murmured, while his mother turned away from the sight and wept. After the father had administered the twelfth stroke he ordered his son to go to his room. The boy left without a word and his mother followed and watched him climb the stairs. She then hurried away to the kitchen and gathered together some olive oil and ointments which she hoped would soothe the pain of her son's wounds. She carried the little jars up to his room, where she found him already in bed. She went over to his side and pulled the sheet back. He turned onto his chest while she prepared the oils. Then she removed his night tunic gently for fear of adding to his pain. Having done so, she stared down at his body in disbelief.

The boy's skin was unmarked.

She ran her fingers gently over her son's unblemished body and found it to be as smooth as if he had just bathed. She turned him over, but there was not a mark on him anywhere. Quickly she covered him with the sheet.

"Say nothing of this to your father, and remove the memory of it from your mind forever, because the very telling of it will only make him more angry."

"Yes, Mother."

The mother leaned over and blew out the candle by the side of the bed, gathered up the unused oils and tiptoed to the door. At the threshold, she turned in the dim light to look back at her son and said:

"Now I know you were telling the truth, Pontius."

THE PRODIGAL DAUGHTER
45685/$3.95
by Jeffrey Archer
The extraordinary national bestseller
by the author of KANE AND ABEL
is finally a paperback!
And You'll Also Love
A QUIVER FULL OF ARROWS
45686/$2.95
also by Jeffrey Archer
POCKET BOOKS
If your bookseller does not have the titles you want, you may order them by sending the retail price (plus 75¢ postage and handling—New York State and New York City residents please add appropriate sales tax) to: POCKET BOOKS, Dept. PRD, 1230 Avenue of the Americas, New York, N.Y. 10020. Send check or money order—no cash or C.O.D.s and be sure to include your name and address. Allow six weeks for delivery. For purchases over $10.00, you may use VISA: card number, expiration date and customer signature must be included.
600